TORQ

911 by Chris C
Bareback by Chr
Bus Stories and Other Tales by Sean Michael • Caged by Sean Michael
Catching a Second Wind by Sean Michael
The Center of Earth and Sky by Sean Michael
Chance Encounters edited by M. Rode • Clear Cut by Alexa Snow
Cowboy Up edited by Rob Knight • Date Night by Kathleen Dale
Demon Princess by Kathleen Dale
Deviations: Submission by Chris Owen and Jodi Payne
Don't Ask, Don't Tell by Sean Michael • Dreams & Daymares by Willa Okati
Dust and Violets by Mike Shade • Farr Anderson Lane by Kathleen Dale
Fine as Frog Hair by Sean Michael • The Floating World by Wheeler Scott Fresh
Starts edited by Rob Knight • Gemini by Chris Owen
A Gentleman of Substance by Julia Talbot
Gods and Monsters by Sean Michael
The Happy Campers by Gale Chester Whittington
Honor Bound by Wheeler Scott • In the Rough by Laura Baumbach
In the Strangest Places by Willa Okati
Jazz and Sapphire by J. Falcon and Kim Burke
Jumping Into Things by Julia Talbot • Keep You by Cindy Rosenthal
Landing with Both Feet by Julia Talbot • Lassoed by BA Tortuga
Latigo by BA Tortuga • The Long Road Home by BA Tortuga
Manners and Means by Julia Talbot • Monsters edited by Rob Knight Mysterious
Ways by Julia Talbot • Myths edited by Rob Knight
Naughty edited by M. Rode • Need by Sean Michael
Night's Kiss by Catherine Lundoff • No Place Like Home by BA Tortuga
Oil and Water by BA Tortuga • One Degree of Separation by Fiona Glass
Out of the Closet by Sean Michael
The Peacock and the Firebird by Julia Talbot • Perfect by Julia Talbot
Personal Best: Going for the Gold by Sean Michael
Playing with Fire by Sean Michael • Post Obsession by Julia Talbot
A Private Hunger by Sean Michael • Rain and Whiskey by BA Tortuga
Second Sight by Sean Michael • Shifting and Shifting Too edited by Rob Knight
The Sound of Your Voice by David Sullivan
The Stallion and the Rabbit by Mike Shade • Stress Relief by BA Tortuga Switched
by Sean Michael • Tempering by Sean Michael
Three Day Passes by Sean Michael • Timeless Hunger by BA Tortuga
Tripwire by Sean Michael • Wheel of Fortune by Julia Talbot
Where Flows the Water by Sean Michael
Winning Hand by Sean Michael

Torquere Press

TOP SHELF
An imprint of Torquere Press Publishers
PO Box 4351
Grand Junction, Colorado 81502

Cover illustration by Plutokitty
Published with permission
ISBN: 1-933389-77-X
www.torquerepress.com

First Torquere Press Printing: October 2005
Printed in the USA

Chapter One

Early evening and the sun was already gone. The hardest days of winter were coming, breathing down the back of his neck like a cold john who just wanted to fuck him over. Trick was out early -- there wasn't anyone looking for a little back-alley fun yet, and it would be hours before the guys in their uptown cars started cruising by.

On the other hand, he was also the only working stiff for five blocks and he walked it like he owned it. If anyone did show, they were his. Which was damned good, because his belly was getting just a little bit on the empty side and being too hungry made you do stupid things.

He walked easily, arms swinging at his sides, pretending he had somewhere to be.

Some sort of new band must be playing at the No Name Bar -- there was already a fucking line. Weird. Trick'd been in there before: watered-down whiskey, crabby bartender, no doors on the bathroom stalls -- he fucking hated blowing a guy in an open-doored stall -- and a cramped, cracked dance floor.

He let his gait slow as he moved past the line; maybe one of them was looking to warm up before seeing the band.

Trick caught the eye of a kid -- fuck, the boy was what? Fourteen? Sixteen if he was a day? Dark purple hair like a goddamned doll, the boy's spare frame was completely encased in skin-tight leather beneath the heavy violet fur coat. He was made up, eyeliner and lipstick, but not girly, not at all. More like an art show -- one of those club kids who spent their lives and their spare change moving from one dance to another. Not a good choice.

Then again, that leather was top-dollar.

He offered the kid a smile, letting his body speak for itself. Trick knew he looked good, all in black, tight t-shirt showing beneath the open leather jacket. Fuck, it was cold.

The interest flared -- and he meant that, it really seemed to change those dark eyes and angled face, but he couldn't tell how. The kid leaned back and spoke to a group of much older players and every single one of them looked over at him as if they shared a brain, looking at him with curiosity.

Well, shit, he didn't mind a threesome, but he wasn't gonna take a whole group -- Benny had been in the hospital for a week after a group wanting blowjobs turned out to be the prelude to getting gangbanged. Still, he let his eyes travel up and down the kid's body, letting him know he was interested in that and sauntered on past the line.

By the time he reached the end of the line without a bite, he figured the new band must be fucking fabulous for these assholes to stand out in the cold. No boot steps followed him, no one hurried after him.

Fuck.

Then a touch came to his elbow and a smooth as fucking glass voice sounded. "So, Sweets. What games do you like to play?"

He turned with a grin. It was the kid. Fuck, but he looked good. Rich and sexy -- Trick could have himself set for the week if this evening went right.

"What have you got in mind?"

"Well, I intend to get laid, but I want to play first." One black eyebrow arched, exposing an eyelid decorated in dozens of sparking colors. "Do you know how to play?"

"I can do getting laid. I can do playing first, too." The kid looked like he was loaded and bored. This could be profitable *and* fun.

"How *very* entertaining." Those dark eyes raked over his body, appreciative and hot. "Limits?"

Limits? Coming from this kid, he nearly laughed, but managed to keep his grin down. "I don't think you need to worry about that."

"No? I think you'd be surprised." The kid held out his leather-gloved hand. "Bast."

This time he did grin. He took the kid's hand, shaking it firmly. "Trick."

That amused the kid, the thin lips curling up, not releasing his hand. "Trick. Unique. I like it. So, what games do you play, Trick?"

"You name it, I'll play it."

Bast turned Trick's hand palm-up, licking a hot, slick line along his lifeline, nipping at the heel of his palm before those eyes met his face, playful and... wicked. "Mm... nice. Hide and seek, I think."

He found himself grinning madly, charmed in spite of himself by this kid. "So who hides and who seeks?"

"I hide and you seek, of course." Slinky and oddly at home in his skin for a kid whose balls could have only been dropped a few years, the kid chuckled, the sound merry. "Do you know where the Clock Tower Club is, Sweets?"

"Over on Bishop? Yeah, I know it." Glitzy, high cover, but good drinks and decent dancing. It wasn't a place most johns wanted to take him.

A thin hand reached into the fur coat and then pressed a $50 bill into his hand. "Go get yourself a nice steak. The game starts at 11:30 tonight. If you seek, then we'll play more. If you don't, then..." Black, black eyes glittered at him. "Well, then we won't."

"That's it? No catches?" This guy was too good to be true.

"Catches are boring, and I don't *do* bored very well." The quick eyes moved again. "Band's starting. Best of luck to you, Sweets. I do hope you're as talented as you taste."

He watched the kid head back to the club, slinking like a cat. Bast didn't bother with the line, heading straight for the bouncer and being let in with little more than a laughing smile.

The kid never looked back.

Trick looked down at the fifty in his hand. Fifty bucks would get him a steak at Carl's House of Steaks, into the club, and he'd still have enough left over for breakfasts for the rest of the week.

Fifty for doing nothing more than talking.

He could turn around and never see the kid again, but the kid was obviously loaded and just wanted to have fun. And he could do fun, especially if it came with a healthy paycheck.

Pocketing the fifty he headed for Carl's, strutting happily, not minding the cold. Not minding it one little bit tonight.

***

The music was blaring, the club packed with sweaty, writhing people slamming against one another, the air thick with smoke. Dark and slick -- once the door shut upon you there was nothing to drive you but the perpetual metallic beat.

Bast was perched atop a column of neon, watching the clock and the crowd and a sweet little redhead with the longest neck he'd seen in decades. Eleven-thirty had passed and his new toy hadn't shown yet.

Disappointing, really. He was quite in the mood to play.

Just as he'd given up, the boy walked in.

Trick was dressed as he had been earlier, becoming almost a shadow in the dark club were it not for his face and hair. He glanced casually about the club before heading for the bar. After speaking to the bartender, he turned back toward the dance floor, one hip resting against the bar.

Bast imagined he could smell the blond. Perhaps he could. He could still taste the salty tang of Trick's palm, tinged with anger and bourbon.

He blended into the background, still and silent as only his kind could be. His hair, clothing, makeup -- it was all slick and metallic and violet and matched the walls and ceilings exactly.

Trick was scanning the crowd, but he did it casually. Bast himself wouldn't have noticed if he hadn't been looking for it. The bartender tapped the kid on the shoulder and Trick twisted, his body outlined briefly in the light as he reached for a shot glass. Strong, lithe muscles twisted beneath the t-shirt and sharp hips bracketed an obvious erection pressing hard against the tight black jeans.

Hunger, sharp and sweet and irresistible, took hold of Bast, grabbed him in fierce jaws and shook him, and it was almost more than he could do to not leap down, plaster himself to the lean body and slake his thirst.

He forced himself to stay still, to stay quiet.

To let his hunger and need build.

Trick tossed back the drink, the long line of his throat exposed, Adam's apple working as he swallowed. The glass was put back on the mirrored bar and Trick turned to the dance floor, once again thrown into shadow.

Bast could see him scanning the crowd again before he sauntered in amongst the dancers, moving to the beat seamlessly, not dancing, almost slinking.

Bast didn't let Trick out of his sight, drinking in the movement of the lithe body. That was why he'd approached the boy -- Trick walked like a predator, some alley cat pretending to be a tiger. It was intriguing as hell.

Trick moved through the dance floor, covering it twice and then circling it as well. His prowling slowed and then stilled altogether, one hand on his hip, a soft frown on his face.

Bast was convinced Trick was about to give up when the blond head suddenly tilted, eyes scanning the neon poles that framed the dance floor. He froze, nipples tightening as he waited to be overlooked or caught. Excitement tasted like fear in his mouth.

Trick's eyes moved past him onto the next column, and on until he'd scanned them all. Bast let his breath out, disappointed, only to freeze again as Trick's eyes came back to the violet column of neon. A smile brightened the handsome face and Trick began to move toward him.

Oh, yes. Good boy. Very, very good boy. He was vibrating with excitement. Nothing tasted as good as a new conquest.

Bast slithered down the column, turning to face Trick, who stood closer than he'd expected. "You found me."

Trick shot a glance to the top of the column and then back to his eyes. Taking a couple of steps forward, Trick crowded him back against the column, the violet light reflected in the blue eyes, making them shimmer. "You blend in pretty well, but your lipstick gave you away – the color is just a touch off."

"Is it? Too red or too blue?" The neon column buzzed against Bast's back, his body responding immediately to the proximity of the hot, firm body.

Trick's head dipped slightly. "Why don't you see for yourself?" The words were whispered against his lips and then Trick's mouth pressed against his, the kiss short but hard.

Lights sparkled behind his eyes as he fought back a groan. Trick pulled back, lips marred with violet paint. Bast reached up and wiped it away, looking down at his fingers. "Too red."

Someone knocked hard into Trick, slamming their bodies together against the column. It felt good, the pressure and heat.

"So, what do you want for your prize?"

Trick grasped the neon pole above his head, bracketing him in, not backing off despite the fact that space had clearly opened up behind him. The lean hips pressed close, the erection Bast had noted earlier hot and hard against him.

"You know what all the guys I pick up say to me? They say 'on your knees, Trick, I want you to suck me.' Well, on your knees, Bast. I want you to suck me."

What a clever boy. Bast had to fight back his grin of sheer delight. Oh yes, this one was something special. Without even a blink, Bast sank to his knees, the neon making his skin positively perfect as Trick watched. His fingers found the zipper of Trick's black jeans and pulled, letting the thick erection spring free.

He could hear Trick's gasp despite the noise of the club, felt the slim hips press forward. "Fuck me..."

Trick's voice was thick with surprise and hot, sharp need.

"But that's not what you claimed as forfeit, Trick." Bast winked up and then slid his slick lips over the head of the swollen cock.

He didn't tease, didn't taunt -- this wasn't the place for that game. Now was the time to feel the bitter pulse of his new boy's seed down his throat, to take his first taste of his Sweets' passion.

Trick's hips shoved his cock deeper, eyes fastened on the meeting of cock and mouth. Two thrusts and Trick was coming, the low groan sweet music to his ears.

Dark -- Trick tasted dark with anger and frustration and incredible need tinged with cheap bourbon and chocolate bars. The need to taste more was intense, and Bast forced himself to let the spent flesh slide from his lips.

He tucked Trick's cock back in the tight jeans and eased the zipper up as he stood. "Forfeit paid."

Bast licked his lips. "You taste good."

Trick backed off only far enough to give him a bit of breathing space. "Yeah? You like that, Bast? You want some more of it?" The cocky words were only slightly softened by the sated look in Trick's eyes.

"I'll take all you're brave enough to offer, Trick." He stretched, beginning to move with the driving beat of the music. "We never did finish that talk about boundaries, Sweets."

Trick's hands left the neon and slid against his shoulders, the boy's body moving with him. "I don't believe in boundaries, Bast. They're... limiting, and I don't like limits."

"No?" Bast closed his eyes in sheer bliss. Oh, Trick *danced*, too. He was definitely keeping hold of this one for a while. "Aren't you worried you'll get hurt?"

"I can take care of myself." Trick's hands slid down to Bast's waist, bringing him back closer to the rangy body, making a show of his strength.

"Oh, I imagine you can." *But oh, couldn't I take better care of you, Sweets.*

"So, you wanna take this somewhere quieter, less..." Trick looked around, hips moving sensuously against Bast's. "Less public?"

"Oh, yes." The temptation to lean forward, to nuzzle his lips against Trick's throat was too much to bear. "I have a place. Walking distance."

Trick's lids dropped half closed. "Perfect."

Then Bast's hand was grabbed and the lithe body moving against his backed off and Trick was leading them off the dance floor and toward the door. Bast followed along, achingly hard, eyes fastened on the sweet, tight ass, stopping only to fetch his coat.

The night air slapped him, icy-cold, as the door opened. "Two blocks north, Sweets. In the warehouses."

Trick hunched against the cold, sliding the tips of his fingers into the tight pockets of his jeans. He would have been warmer if he'd done up the leather jacket he wore, but Bast imagined it would take a far colder night than this one for Trick to admit to being cold. "The warehouses? Not much living up here, 'specially at night."

"It has its appeal. Nice open space, room for the music to bounce, and those of us who live there respect each other's privacy. Handy, when you live on the edge of night." His voice sounded deep, echoing hollowly in his own head, hunger sharp as steel knives against bone. "Would you be more comfortable somewhere else? Somewhere more public and less... quiet?"

Trick managed to shrug without his fingers coming out of his pockets. "It's your dime, Bast. If you wanna do it in public, though, it's gonna cost you extra."

He could feel his eyebrows arch, feel the low scratch of irritation at the base of his spine. He kept forgetting this one was a whore, didn't really want to play. Odd. Not as odd as him picking up rent boys, but odd. Bast wrinkled his nose.

Oh well, one night. One fuck and a bit of a nibble and tomorrow he'd go hunt someone more willing. "Well, how much extra is sucking you off at the club going to cost? Or did the fact that I paid your cover at the door take care of it?"

Trick shrugged again, looking a bit uncomfortable. "That was my prize, right? Most guys aren't into being the ones doing the sucking, you know?" Trick flashed him a smile, but it looked forced. "I don't mind it really, I just don't like audiences. Changes the dynamics."

Bast nodded and continued walking towards his building. He was tempted just to pay the kid off and send him home. He had a few little toys that were always willing to slake his thirst -- they weren't a challenge, but a meal was a meal. "It does. If you don't mind, I'd rather do this at my place, rather than a hotel. I don't do mornings and would rather have my own space."

"Sure. I don't usually stay the night, but I can if you want." Trick sounded more sure of himself now.

"We'll wing it. Regardless, I'll get you a cab home. I'll be dead to the world come morning." The pun amused Bast, almost restored his earlier humor.

Sometimes he yearned for older days, when this process required little more than a good manservant and a decent title. Then again, chamber music and reading by candlelight were utterly overrated and, although manservants were hard to come by, 'net chat rooms were almost as effective.

"I don't like mornings myself," Trick confided as he kicked a can out into the street. "Nothing worse than the sun hitting you in the face when you aren't ready to face the world yet."

"No shit." Reaching the large, silent warehouses surrounded by the bleak iron fence, Bast swiped his key card at the gate and then hurried through. "Come on in. I'm in the back. I have the basement level in that smaller warehouse with the mural."

"That's a pretty cool mural." Trick had his hands out of his pockets now and his arms were swinging easily at his sides. The predatory walk was back, the cold not so noticeable once they were indoors. "Have you ever seen the ghost?"

"Hmm?" Bast hurried forward, opening up the series of locked doors that led to the elevator grate. The key was in his hand, the ancient elevator making loud grunts and ticks as it forced itself to the ground level. "Which ghost?"

"Rumor has it there's a ghost around here -- one of DiMaco's boys was dealing out 'round the mural and he claimed someone was stealing his stuff and spooking him out. We told him it had to be the competition, but he claimed there was noises when there was nobody there to make 'em and stuff." Trick laughed. "You gotta admit a ghost is way cooler than some guy wanting to horn in on DiMaco's territory."

Bast grinned. "Absolutely, Sweets. You into the scene then? You don't seem the type."

Bast watched carefully. The boy wasn't into dope; he would've tasted it on Trick's skin, on his seed. It flavored a person, sweet to bitter, depending. The interesting question was, would Trick lie?

Trick almost flinched for a split second before he covered it under an easy-going, if somewhat false smile. "Nah, not my scene. I don't mind living in the streets but that don't mean I wanna sleep in the gutter, you know?"

Interesting.

"I much prefer living in my little flat, thank you. I know what you mean, though. There are things much more fun than what you can find on the street." He opened the elevator and motioned Trick in. "Two flights down."

"Two?" Trick laughed. "You really are underground, aren't you?"

"As much as I can be, yeah." The elevator wheezed and groaned all the way down, the blue light bulb flickering. "I swear, I'm gonna start taking the stairs."

"I don't know -- there's worse places to get stuck than in an elevator." Trick pushed him back against the wall and rubbed against him, tongue flicking out to slide across his lips. "Going down?"

"I believe I've already shown my skill in that arena, Sweets." Bast slid his hand over the bulge beneath Trick's zipper, letting the tip of his tongue touch Trick's for a second. "But you were quite delectable."

"Oh, yeah, you were pretty fucking good." Trick's smile was cocky. "I'm not so bad myself, so you know, if we get caught in this clunker we'll have plenty to entertain ourselves with."

Bast arched an eyebrow as the elevator settled. "Practice makes perfect, or so they tell me. We're here. Welcome to my home, Trick."

The grate opened into the dark, slick room Bast called home. The lamps were low, the violet light sliding over the curves and angles of furniture and assorted wrought iron sculptures. Simple, perfect -- the eyes immediately drawn to the huge velvet draped bed, a single spotlight trained on the painting that hung above it.

Electricity was such a wonderful thing.

The painting contained a slim, pale, androgynous figure draped in a red cloth, face hidden except for the single tear-stained cheek kissed by the moon's light. White marble statues surrounded the person, making the figure seem surreal and otherworldly, flushed with life.

"Wow." Trick wandered around the room, hands trailing over the sculptures before heading to the bed. "This is a damn fine place to live."

"It's not bad. I like it. Suits my needs." Shrugging off his coat and gloves, Bast wandered over to the bar, opening the low, sleek cabinet. Odd and post-modern, the furniture amused him, with its long lines and interesting colors and curves. In fact, Trick would be lovely bound and gagged on the low red divan, moaning in ecstasy. Pure art.

"Want a drink?"

"Yeah, sure."

Trick was sitting on the bed, testing its bounce. The boy's fingers kept returning to the velvet drapery, smoothing over the soft material.

"Bourbon, yes?" He nodded over to the bed before grabbing up a bottle and pouring a finger of bourbon into a cut crystal glass. "It's a silly indulgence, but I like how it feels on my skin."

"I'll bet." Trick was checking out the rest of the room from the vantage of the bed, but his fingers stayed with the velvet.

Bast wandered over to the bed and handed Trick the glass. Then he settled at the end of the bed, pulling off the shiny thigh boots and bright vest. Covered now only in soft, textured fabric that clung and shimmered and caressed his skin like a glove, Bast relaxed, sighing soft and easy. "That's better."

Trick poured the bourbon back in a single shot, put his glass on the floor, and then looked him over. Bast could feel his eyes as they wandered up his body.

Trick looked around the place again before focusing back on him. "Can I ask you a question?"

"Ask away." That fascinating rush of curiosity rushed through Bast again, making him tingle.

"You're obviously rich. You're great looking, you could have anybody you wanted -- why'd you pick me up?"

"You're interesting. You smell good. I like the way you walk." Bast grinned. "I didn't know you were a pro. I was just looking for someone to have fun with."

"I'm not really a pro -- it's not like I got anyone running me or nothing, but why give it away for free, you know? A bit of fun is nice but it doesn't put steak in your belly."

Bast nodded -- he understood about trading your body for goods, had practiced it often and willingly. He just wanted a willing playmate, someone who wanted the sensation, the challenge. "I just saw you, you know? Just like you saw me. I thought you were interesting. It's not very often I see someone interesting. Speaking of steak, did you go get one this evening?"

Trick grinned at him. "Oh yeah. You were more than generous -- went to a place where it's good enough to have nice and rare, swimming in blood once you cut it. Man, I almost licked the plate clean."

The hunger flared again, ripping through Bast's stomach like a razor. He looked down, knowing that his eyes would have gone feral, bright and glowing softly. His voice deepened, smoothed, took on a silky tone. "I should have been there to appreciate it."

He closed his eyes, praying to all the long-dead gods that Trick would be still and quiet until the need passed.

"Yeah, nothing like a good steak. Woulda been nice not to have to eat alone." The bed shifted as Trick got up. Bast could hear the booted feet wander around, hands sliding over furniture and sculptures. Could hear the thrum-thrum-thrum slide of blood through living veins and arteries and organs. "So you want me to stay, Bast? We gonna have some fun?"

"Oh, yes. I want you, Sweets. You make me hungry." Bast swallowed hard against the need, burying it deep, and looked up, meeting Trick's eyes. "What about you? You want to play with me?"

"Oh yeah..." Trick kicked off his boots and stripped off his jacket before climbing back onto the bed and straddling Bast's hips. "Let's play."

The boy leaned forward, lips against his, tongue pressing, asking for admittance. Bast opened to Trick, letting himself be kissed and touched, his focus on controlling his need. Trick was heavy against him, hot and hard, the smell of semen and bourbon and blood wafting in the air.

Trick's tongue surged into his mouth, sliding along his teeth and tangling with his tongue. One of Trick's hands slid into his hair, angling his head and sliding his mouth sideways, changing the kiss as Trick's tongue slid deeper.

He pulled Trick's t-shirt out from the waistband, hands moving to trail over the warm skin, tracing muscles that jumped for him, leapt up into his touch. He moaned into Trick's mouth, hips pushing up.

Trick pushed back, the motion rolling, rhythmic, pressing their erections together, the bite of Trick's zipper cold through his skintight clothes.

Bast was awash with need, hungry as if he hadn't fed both passion and thirst with a sweet young thing with blood like cheap wine and strawberries only hours ago. It was terrifying, agonizing, unbearably exciting.

The mouth feeding from his pulled away as Trick slid the zipper of Bast's catsuit down and pushed the material off his chest. Trick's hot mouth closed over one of his nipples, teeth grazing and tongue sliding hot and wet.

Bast watched as Trick nibbled and suckled at his skin. The curve of Trick's neck was bared, close and throbbing with life, calling with a steady low wail - oboe solos in an empty concert hall. Bast traced the fine line with one finger, cock swelling impossibly at the pulse beneath his touch.

Or maybe like the scream of a thin-lipped punker, backed by nothing but a snare and a beat-up Les Paul.

Trick slid the zipper down further, fingers beneath it, making sure it slid smoothly over his cock. The warm skin slid against him, just a tease, and then disappeared again once his suit was completely unzipped.

"Oh, Sweets, you make me ache." Bast tugged the dark cotton t-shirt off Trick's chest, hands ranging over the hot-smooth skin.

Trick's eyes met his as Trick arched into his touch; they were full of passion and hunger. "I know the feeling."

He groaned, surging up so his body met Trick's, hissing at the heat and pleasure that filled him. He ducked his head against the hard shoulder, letting his open mouth trail over blood pumping close to the surface. Symphonies. He could hear symphonies pounding away inside those veins. "Who are you, Sweets? What magic do you hold?"

"I'm Trick -- told you I was good." The cocky words were spoken somewhat breathlessly, one of Trick's hands twisting his nipple, the other sliding down between them toward his cock.

"Want you. Hungry..." So close, Bast could feel the life, right there, right beneath his tongue and this one would taste so sweet, so good. "Oh..."

"Oh yeah." Trick's hand circled his cock and began to stroke him, pulling strong and steady. "Let me fuck you, Bast? I'll make you feel so good."

"Yes. Want to feel you inside me." Bast groaned, fingers tangling within Trick's hair. The temptation to tilt the boy's head and draw that fascinating rhythm into himself was painful. "Want to feel you deep."

"Yeah, that's right, deep inside you." Trick shifted, pulling them up and then beginning to work his skintight suit off. "Trick'll take care of you."

"Will you? You sure about that, Sweets? Sure you can ease my ache?" Bast slithered out of his clothes, sighing as the air replaced the fabric in caressing his skin. He slowly pumped his own cock, stretching so Trick's eyes traveled over his naked body.

"That's what you're paying me for, isn't it?" Trick's fingers popped the button on his jeans, slid down his zipper, and then hooked through a pair of loops, pulling the tight, black material down slim hips. "Gonna make you feel so good, Bast."

"So you've said. So come here and fuck me, Sweets. We're burning moonlight."

The mention of money had splashed against his nerves like ice water, his ego balking at the thought that he wasn't being admired or wanted -- not for his looks or his gifts or his skill. This boy was cheap rent and wasn't interested in anything but cash. Time to get this particular transaction done and find someone willing. They always tasted sweeter on the palette.

He almost growled at the loss of Trick's melody.

Trick's mouth was on his again, body pushing him back onto the bed. One hand slid beneath his arm and around his back, pulling him up into the middle of the bed.

Just as quickly his legs were being spread, a finger slick with lube pressing against him, teasing against his skin and then pushing in. Bast relaxed, rocking up into the touch, reminding himself with each motion that Trick didn't want this, didn't want him, that the swirling void of hunger wouldn't be filled by this one, no matter what his body insisted.

Trick's fingers kept him busy enough that he almost didn't notice Trick sliding a condom over his cock, and then the blunt head was pressing against him. He tilted his head back, eyes focused on the painting above the bed. His hips tilted, pressure filling him, forcing his eyes closed. The bright color amongst the white stone danced in his mind, teasing him with promises and lies and whispers of forever and hunger.

Promises that never came true, never had and never would and he wanted the music back, goddamnit.

Trick didn't stop until he was buried completely inside Bast, and then he stopped moving, waiting and still. Every now and then his head would dip and flick across one nipple or the other, the touch teasing, taunting.

Something deep and dark and feral within Bast snapped. This *child* teasing him, taunting him, acting like he was some needy, hungry animal. Allowing himself to move freely, Bast flipped them, sinking back onto Trick's cock with a hiss. He pressed down on Trick's shoulders, beginning to ride the flesh within him, feeding the ache within him -- fucking instead of being fucked.

Trick's hands grabbed his waist, legs coming up, hips tilting as he dug his heels into the bed. Trick pushed up into each downward movement, hands adding force, refusing to give up all the control to Bast.

Using everything he'd learned in centuries of debauchery, Bast worked his body, fighting to make Trick scream, to make this something the boy would dream about, ache for, need deep within his soul.

Trick's eyes had closed and his breath was coming in short, sharp gasps, his thighs trembling against Bast's buttocks and lower back. One hand slid around Bast's waist to wrap around his erection.

Bast reached down and tilted Trick's head, exposing the smooth line of throat. Silently, he dipped his head, razor-sharp teeth sliding out quickly to pierce the fine skin.

He heard Trick's cry of pleasure, feeling the body beneath him convulse as wave after wave of erotic sensation crashed against overwrought nerves. Then the thick sweetness of Trick's blood filled his mouth -- so good, less bitter than the boy's seed, thicker, full of life, so fucking hot and full of harmony...

Trick shuddered beneath him a few times and then grew still, breathing like he'd been running for miles.

Bast licked gently, tongue soothing the wounds into soft pink spots, flesh closing easily. Need sated, he leaned back, feeling his body grow flush and heavy with blood. "You okay, Sweets?"

Trick propped himself up on his elbows. "Shit, yeah, that was pretty fucking intense." He fell back onto the bed with a sigh. "Looks like you're going to want your money back though."

"Oh, now, I wouldn't do that to a working boy." Bast stood, Trick's cock sliding free from him. He moved across the room, walking unselfconsciously and gracefully to his wallet. "Will $500 cover your trouble and your cab fare?"

Silence met his question, and he looked back at Trick to find the boy staring at him with his mouth hanging open. "Five hundred dollars and you didn't even get off?"

Then Trick was shaking his head and getting up off of the bed. "Yeah, $500'll do fine."

"Wonderful." Bast counted out the money and handed it over before turning on the stereo. Vivaldi was playing, the notes not strong enough to erase Trick's song from inside his head, so he flipped it to the Toxic Spills. His makeup was smeared and uncomfortable and he needed a nice, hot shower. "The phone's over by the door. Feel free."

He wandered over to the bar and poured himself a glass of sweet port, the sugared wine clinging to the sides of the crystal in long streaks.

"That's okay, I'll find something on the street." Trick was sliding back into his clothes with practiced efficiency.

Bast nodded, drinking down the wine quickly, letting the sweetness cover up the bitter aftertaste of lust. "Don't spend it all in one place, Sweets, and be careful. There are ghosts out there."

Trick snorted as he pulled on his jacket. "Right." He made his way over to the elevator and stood a moment, hand ready to pull across the grating. "It's not the ghosts that can hurt you, Bast."

"No, I don't suppose they can." Bast allowed himself a heartbeat of regret and then pushed it away. "It was lovely playing with you, Sweets. You're something special."

"Oh yeah -- you had a real good time, I could tell." The words were self-depreciating and contained a hint of apology. Trick pulled the grate shut, calling out before the elevator started to move. "You know where to find me."

"Yes. 'Night, Trick." Bast felt vaguely ill and empty, turning his back as the elevator gears began to whine, and he turned Rose's whiskey and ashes voice up to cover it.

***

He'd called Bael before the last song on the CD faded. "Hey, pretty boy, 's Bast. I need you."

Bael hadn't argued, hadn't complained, hadn't mentioned the time or the inconvenience, simply murmured "Yeah, babe. 'm on my way."

Bast hung up the phone, wandering over to the bed and looking at Bryce's painting. "It doesn't get easier, you know? Wanting someone like you."

With a sigh, he wandered into the bathroom, the black marble cold upon his feet. No mirrors; Bast had no use for them, and the reminder of his biological peculiarities tended to startle his lovers. He turned off the lights and turned on the shower and stepped in, moaning as the heat surrounded him. He ached, still hard, still hungry, wine like bile in his mouth. Damn the boy, anyway.

Damn his song, too.

His soap smelled of dark woods and moss, heat and lather washing away Bast's false face, leaving him pale and stark against the tile. His hair slid around him, touching his skin. He stroked himself slowly, moaning and arching through the steam.

"Fuck, Bast, you're sex made flesh." The soft southern drawl hit him a second before lips covered his cock, Bael taking him in deep, sucking him strongly, hands moving over his skin.

"Mm... pretty boy. Need you." Bast arched, pressing deep into the welcoming heat. Bael's skin, ebony against his own, was lovely in the darkness. Bast could see the life, the hunger pulsing within the man. Eyes as black as his own glanced up, a sweet need buried within them and he came with a cry, tension releasing its hold from his body, welcome silence filling his head.

Bael suckled him for a long moment before standing and pulling him close, resting his head against a willing throat. "Feed, babe, and then we'll play. I haven't screamed for you in too long."

Yes. Bast felt his eyes go hot, and he took a long lick of damp skin before biting deep.

Oh, yes.

***

The cold hit Trick as soon as he opened the warehouse door, and he had a half a mind to settle in a corner of the hall and spend the night, but instinct told him Bast wouldn't take too kindly to his evening guest cluttering up the hall come morning.

He slipped all but one twenty down the front of his jeans and zipped up his leather jacket. Shoving his hands as far into his jeans as he could, he made his way back downtown. It was a long walk, but he didn't want to pay some cab driver a penny when he had two perfectly good legs.

Dawn was pressing at the night sky when he hit Roman Street, and he headed for Rosie's All Nighter for a Coke and some breakfast. He sat at the counter, jacket undone, slowly warming up. Old Sid was the only other one in the place besides the waitress, his smelly carcass down at the other end of the counter. There'd be more folks soon -- a few night shifters coming for a meal before they hit their beds, others having a cup of coffee before starting their day, but for now it was quiet and warm.

The Coke was cold and he chewed on the ice; he liked the way it crunched beneath his teeth, the sound kind of echoing around his mouth and ears. It almost drowned out the Christmas music that was playing over the diner's speakers. It wasn't Christmas time. It wasn't even close, just a miserable early March day, but the diner only ever played Christmas music.

He'd finished his first Coke and was partway through the second when his plate was plunked down in front of him. The eggs were over hard and greasy. Everything was greasy, the potatoes, the bread, the bacon and sausages. It tasted better than it looked, but it made him think of Carl's where he'd had his steak last night. Food there tasted good and looked good; the people that ate there looked good, too, with their hair all pretty and their clothes neat and dressy.

Of course if he wanted to eat in places like that more often he was going to have to smarten up. If he'd played his cards right he could have had Bast eating out of his hand. A nice warm place to stay, clothes, food.

Even as he thought about it though, he grimaced. He wasn't cut out to be anyone's kept boy. He could handle the sex, he liked the sex, and Bast sure as hell seemed good at it. Fuck, he'd never come so hard. But how could he walk down the streets, knowing everyone who saw him knew that he was living off this guy?

"You've got too much fucking pride, boy. Don't worry, I'll beat it out of you."

That had been Josef, one of a parade of boyfriends his mom had brought home. Looked like Josef hadn't quite beaten him long or hard enough.

Well, he had five hundred bucks in his jeans. It should keep him in warm breakfasts until the weather got warm again, and he wouldn't have to go back to the house until fall. If he kept up a little back-alley blow job business, he could eat pretty well, maybe even have some saved up to make it through to Christmas and not go see

Mom before that. She usually managed to lose the boyfriend right before the holidays.

He'd just have to forget about guys with olive skin and hair that looked purple who could fuck like nobody he'd ever done before. After all, he was pretty damn sure Bast had forgotten about him.

The bell on the door rang and the waitress called out to the two men that strolled through.

"The usual, boys?"

"Thanks, Roni."

Trick picked up his fork and dug into his breakfast.

Chapter Two

"Bael, my pretty boy, you should *always* wear white." The club was jumping, lines of brightly-dressed peacocks circling the block. Buoyant and generally pleased with the world, Bast was sated, the moon was full, the July night was balmy, and the Toxic Spills were playing a late set.

Bast let his hand trail along ebony skin draped in a sheer blousy shirt, which was already heavy with the humidity in the air. He tweaked the hard nipple and winked at the gasp his friend and sometime-lover gave. "Going in or coming out?"

"Coming out, of course." Bael chuckled, arm draping over a glittery girl with a bald head and a tattoo of a snarling tiger on her cheek. "We're going to find a more private party. Wanna?"

He shook his head, the newly blackened hair flowing over his shoulders like raw silk, rasping against the tight vinyl cat suit he'd poured himself into. "Need to party, pretty boy. Need to dance."

Disappointment lit the dark brown eyes briefly, and then Bael gave him a saucy smile. "Well, if you change your mind or need something you can't find elsewhere..."

His attention was caught by a familiar voice raised in anger. "Come on, you *know* me, Blake. I can't believe you're going to play me like this."

"Sweets." The name was out of his mouth before he could stop it. Bast turned, eyes trailing over the black-clad body, imagining the heat of the skin beneath.

"See something you like, babe?" Bael's voice was warm and teasing, hot mouth coming to rest beside Bast's beringed ear. "He's not free trade, lover. You know that, right?"

"Oh, yeah. I know." Bast smiled, nuzzling against Bael's cheek. "I like the way he smells, Bael. He's a sharp one."

"And what Bast likes..." Bael's warm laughter finished the thought and then Bast's attention was caught again by the boy arguing with the bouncer.

"Oh, hey, come on! I was next in line." Trick threw his hands in the air as the bouncer let the couple behind him into the club. "I can't fucking believe you're doing this to me."

Bast sauntered up to the door, giving a brief wave to Bael's retreating form. He pushed his way through the throng up to the bouncer, letting his hand wrap around Blake's bulging bicep. "Hey there. Did you hold a space for me?"

Blake looked down into his eyes and smiled and opened the velvet rope. "Of course, Bast. So good to see you. Rose will be so pleased you came to see her sing."

"Don't forget my date, Blake." Bast looked back at Trick, hand firm against the bouncer's. "I told you I'd be here, Sweets. You should trust I wouldn't leave you out in the cold. Or the heat, as the case may be."

Trick blinked at him and for a moment Bast thought the boy was going to blow it, but then he smiled and shrugged. "I was late -- I figured I'd missed you."

He tossed his hair and smiled brilliantly at Blake. "They never appreciate how long it takes to look this good. Come on, Sweets. Take me dancing."

He held his hand out and smiled as Trick's slid into it. Then they were both in, Blake with a nice tip slipped into a back pocket. The lights and the music hit them as soon as they stepped in, and Trick's hand was warm in his.

Trick pressed close behind him. "Thanks. I'd hate to have missed the Toxics."

Bast grinned. "No problem. Listening to Rose is like listening to an angel -- well, a really, really hoarse, chain-smoking, whiskey-drenched angel with kick-ass tattoos."

The beat was throbbing, moving through him like the pulse of a heartbeat. He could feel Trick start to move behind him, body swaying in time with the beat.

"Oh, yeah. I could come just listening to her."

"You wouldn't be the first, Sweets. I can remember listening to her wailing down in an old dive in the barrios -- she had hair then, black as night." He raised his face as a familiar face passed close -- Melody, maybe, or Gennie, he wasn't sure -- a soft kiss dropping on his lips. "Listening to her was like fucking on an icy bridge."

"An icy bridge? I'm not sure that sounds like too much fun. Look, if you were meeting someone, I'll just do my own thing -- I really appreciate the in, but I don't want to cramp your style."

"Hmm? Meeting someone?" Bast turned, a soft smile on his face, body moving to the beat. "Nah, I just came for the music. And being close to a hot body when the icy wind is blowing can be a trip."

"Oh yeah?" Trick moved with him, body close, sliding sensuously with the music.

"Yeah. With the right body, it can send you flying." Bast let himself relax, let his instincts and the music and Trick lead his motions. Trick smiled down at him and slowly moved them into the center of the floor, where they were forced closer together by the crowd.

"You're one hell of a dancer, Sweets." Bast sighed as Trick's body brushed against him. It felt good, warm and comfortable, the tension of their previous meeting eased by time and the seductive rhythm of Trick's heart.

Bast grinned at himself. The fact that he'd fed well before heading out into the night didn't hurt either.

"I was just thinking the same thing about you." Trick's hands slid over his shoulders and slowly down his back until Trick was cupping his ass. The driving beat seemed suddenly more intimate as Trick brought their groins together.

"Oh..." Bast let himself meet Trick's eyes for a moment and then his lids fell closed, body undulating beneath Trick's hands.

He could feel Trick's eyes on him, heavy like a physical touch.

The music changed, slowed and Trick pulled him closer, hips slowing to match the music. Bast let his hands circle Trick's neck, the beat sensual, sexual. So often, dancing was simply a precursor to fucking, a way to show off, birds preening in the hopes that their plumage would catch an interested eye. Dancing with Trick was... dancing.

Trick bent his head to whisper in his ear. "Do you do everything as well as you dance and fuck?"

"I can't play pool worth a damn." Silver-bright sparkles lit behind his eyes, the rich warmth of Trick's body pouring through him, ending heavy and dense in his balls. "Oh, and I never learned how to swim."

"I could teach you sometime, if you wanted. Pool the table not pool the water." Trick's breath continued warm against his neck. "It's a fun game. All those balls..."

Bast chuckled. "Not to mention leaning over a table, rubbing that blue stuff -- chalk, isn't it? -- on the soft tips of sticks. Sounds very interesting. I'd like to learn." He leaned back and winked. "Then I'd only have to learn to swim to be good at everything."

Trick chuckled, the laughter rubbing his body against Bast's in a movement counter to the smooth slide of their dance.

Someone bumped into Bast, pushing him hard into Trick's body, nose slamming into Trick's chin. Lights sparked behind Bast's eyes for a second and he swayed, Trick's arms keeping him upright.

"Damn it!" he growled, shaking his head. "You okay, Sweets?"

"Yeah, I'm fine. You? You hit me pretty hard." One of Trick's hands left his ass and slid over his face, fingers gentle across his nose.

Bast lifted his face, letting the touch soothe him. "I think I'll live. No blood?" He lifted his chin further, lips almost close enough for a kiss.

"No blood." Trick's lips brushed his as he spoke, voice gone husky.

"Oh, good." Bast couldn't have said if he meant the lack of blood or the tingle Trick's lips left behind. He reached up, touched the strong chin with a single finger. "Doesn't look any the worse for wear, either."

"I think I'll live." Trick's tongue came out and slid over the tip of Bast's finger.

"I think that's a good plan, Sweets. You're one of the most alive people I've ever seen." Bast smiled, finger tracing over the full lips. He wanted to kiss those lips, wanted another taste of Trick, but he didn't want to break the natural, easy spell the music had woven around them.

Trick nibbled on the end of his fingertip and then pulled it into his mouth, sucking softly. Their hips were still moving together, following a rhythm all their own now.

His breath was caught in his chest, still and dead, his focus on Trick's face -- hot lips and flashing eyes. The club had disappeared, the other dancers fading. Only Trick and the music were left, alive and pulsating.

Trick let Bast's finger slide from his mouth. "Shit." Lips covered his own, soft but firm, hungry.

Bast opened to the kiss, a soft moan vibrating between them. Trick tasted as rich and addictive as he remembered -- less bitter, more sweet and somehow deep.

They were bumped again and their teeth hit, Trick's lip splitting open. His tongue slid over the split, at once healing the tiny cut and letting the bright taste of blood burst inside him. Then he backed away, looking into Trick's eyes. "You okay?"

Trick nodded, tongue flicking out over his lip where the scratch had been. "It's starting to get dangerous out here. I don't suppose... I guess after all the fuss to get it in would be rude to leave before Toxics' set."

Bast shrugged and flashed Trick a quick grin. "They won't miss us, and if the crowds trample us we'll miss the show anyway." He took a deep breath, took a chance. "You interested in taking a walk, maybe getting a cup of coffee?"

"Yeah, I guess I am." The words themselves weren't very enthusiastic, but the tone they were uttered in spoke of surprised want and need.

"Cool." Bast smiled, warm and relaxed and inexcusably pleased. "Let's blow this joint and find some java."

Trick grinned and then slipped an arm over one of Bast's shoulders, draping over him like a cloak, and wound them through the crowd.

They found their way out, Bast's eyes moving automatically to the sky to gauge the possible coming of dawn. He'd been doing it for years - wrist sundials being bulky and heavy and well, only available in cartoons and badly-written Saturday Night Live skits -- although he knew when the sun rose, had rarely been caught short. It was his habit.

The moon was wicked bright, the closest Bast could remember to daylight. "Oh, man. She's a beauty, isn't she?"

Trick, still half hanging over him, looked around. "Where?"

He pointed up into the silvered face of the closest thing he had to a god. "The moon. It's full."

Head tilting, Trick looked up. The moon caressed his skin, making his lips and eyes shine. "'S nice."

"Yes. She is." Bast admired Trick for a second and then he scanned the street, looking for a place with decent music and better than decent coffee. "How about Hannah's? The coffee's rich and the booths aren't lumpy."

"Sure -- they've got a fantastic pecan pie there, too." Trick detached himself from around Bast, taking his hand instead.

Bast wandered with him down the busy street. They were stopped often. This was Bast's second home and where he loved to play, after all, and he was well-liked and well-known. He introduced Trick to everyone who stopped them, making sure to keep the atmosphere light and friendly. The last thing he wanted was to make the boy uncomfortable.

Bast liked Trick, liked the smell of him, the feel of him. Liked the fire and just-banked passion. Liked the music of the steady heartbeat. Even if they were just friends, Bast sensed great fun slept beneath that nonchalant mien.

By the time they made it to Hannah's, Trick was shaking his head. "Is there anyone you don't know?" he asked as he opened the door for Bast.

He chuckled. "Not around here, Sweets. I'm a bit of a fixture on this block. Move two blocks east and no one knows my name."

He hurried in, grinning at Trick's laugh, as Hannah herself stood, brushing her hands on her apron and called out, "Sebastian! Lovely! Your usual? There's a booth open in the back."

Trick slid into the booth across from him, his easy sprawl taking up most of the booth and ensuring that one leg was pressed against his own. "So what were you doing on Roman Street?"

"Heard there was a new group playing at the No Name Bar, a bit dark, a bit loud, but with some killer bass and a sweet-voiced thing doing harmony." Bast shrugged and grinned, resting his chin on his propped up hands. "I'm very into music."

Hannah waddled over, about ready to pop with another one of her brood. "So, boys, what's your poison? And Sebastian, why haven't you been in lately? You cheating on me with one of those Starbucks floosies?"

"Me? Cheat on your coffee? Not a chance!" Bast laughed and patted her swollen stomach. "Coffee, black, dark, hot, please."

"I take mine black, too, and a really big piece of pecan pie."

Hannah nodded and waddled off, looking back over her shoulder. "I liked the red hair better, Bast. The black's too stark with that skin of yours."

Trick shook his head. "The purple was best."

"I liked the purple, too, but I needed a change. Besides, it would have clashed with this outfit, and an outfit like this deserves to be worn once or twice a year."

"I'll give you that." Trick shifted, leg hot against his, hand coming out to slide along his chest, the look in Trick's eyes hot and needy.

"You like it? It's warm inside, clings, you know? So you never quite forget you're wearing it." Bast let his leg move against Trick's, knowing he lied. He had forgotten, at the club, dancing with Trick. He hadn't remembered the clothes at all.

"Oh, yeah, I know that it clings." Trick's voice had gone low, husky. Bast could smell his arousal.

His belly tightened, rippled, and he was suddenly sure Trick could see the motion through the vinyl -- could see his nipples harden, the goosebumps along his arms, the swell of his cock in the shadows.

"Suddenly I don't feel so much like coffee and pie..."

"No?" Bast touched Trick's hand, eyes closing for a second at the smooth warmth, the pulse beneath his fingers.

Trick's hand turned in his, fingers tickling along his palm. "I'm hungry... but not for coffee."

"Come home with me?" Bast looked at Trick, meeting need with need. Trick nodded slowly, fingers twining with his. Bast nodded back, turning to look at Hannah. "Make it to go?"

Hannah nodded and slid the pie into a plastic box, poured the coffee into white to-go cups, and they slid out of the booth. Bast left a ten on the table and then they were heading out the door. Trick's arm slid around his waist, the boy's hip bumping against his with every step.

Bast murmured softly, the warmth of Trick's body leaching into him, making his joints loose and easy, walking almost as good as dancing.

The moon led them home.

Trick was quiet, but his body spoke for him; he wanted this.

The elevator rumbled up, and Bast handed his cup to Trick and lifted the grate without a word. Together they entered, and Bast took Trick's hand as they descended.

Trick let his hand go and passed his coffee over along with the boxed pie, eyes meeting his. "Going down?" Trick slid to his knees, body pressing along Bast's and then he began to mouth Bast through the skin-tight vinyl.

"Oh." A tremor moved through his body, the heat and pressure of Trick's tongue against him sending him flying with the promise of that mouth on his skin. His hands full of hot coffee, he could only stand and enjoy, little soft cries of pleasure and encouragement pouring from him.

"Fuck, but you smell good." Trick was looking up at him, cheek rubbing against his cock. "That's what I remember most from that night. I'll be minding my own business, just walking along the street, and then I'll catch a hint of ... something and all of a sudden I'm thinking about being buried inside you, and still somehow being the one getting fucked." Head turning, Trick licked the outline of his cock, almost desperate in his movements.

"I can't shake the way you tasted -- I dream about it, dream about the taste of your lips, your cock, your throat." The elevator stopped and Bast lifted his chin, savoring the shivers moving through his body. "Come on, Sweets. The bed's soft and warm and big enough to explore on."

Trick stood and opened the grate, leading the way across the room. He stopped halfway to the bed and turned, a soft, shy smile on his face. "The coffee's going to get cold."

"We'll nuke it or we'll make more or we'll drink it cold." Bast grinned, setting the food down and moving over to feel the comfort of Trick's heat. "The pie will keep, and that's the best part, right?"

Trick slid his arms around Bast's waist and shook his head. "No. This is." The kiss was warm and sweet and full of hunger.

Bast met the kiss wholeheartedly, losing himself in the tastes of hunger and need and fear and want. The ferocity and fury of the other night was eased, each kiss growing warmer and deeper, Trick beginning to make delicious little noises against his lips. He pressed close with a soft moan, almost coming in his clothes as another flavor introduced itself. Pleasure. The sweet-rich flavor rocketed within him, addictive as heroin in his veins.

Trick's hands slid down to cup his ass, pulling him against sharp hips and hard cock, rubbing them together. Bast's hands found Trick's hair, sinking deep into the thick silk. Every inch of his skin was awake, aware, alive. He pressed into Trick's hips, adding his motions to their dance. He wanted skin on skin, but he didn't want to stop, wasn't sure he could stop. Trick whimpered and the kisses became deeper, almost desperate as their hips moved urgently together, sliding and rubbing and pressing, and Trick was hard like steel.

Bast came with a sharp cry, eyes flashing open as his body convulsed, heat spreading at his groin.

Trick kept them moving a moment or two longer and then he came too, with a long hard jerk.

Bast lifted his head, took another slow, sweet kiss, refusing to let Trick's regret take hold in the absence of need. The edge was off, but he wanted -- no, needed -- more, skin and tongue and cock and Trick.

"I don't think I've come in my pants since I was a kid."

Bast grinned. "I won't tell on you if you don't tell on me."

Trick grinned at that. "It's a deal. So... that outfit has to be pretty uncomfortable right now."

"Yeah." Bast chuckled and winked. "Pretty damned. In fact, I'm thinking I might need a shower. There's got to be come from my knees to my armpits."

Trick laughed, the sound light. "That's the price you pay for wearing those tight, slinky outfits."

"No, the real price is trying to not explain what the stains are to the dry cleaner." Bast rolled his eyes and wrinkled his nose. "Those? Oh, they're... milk. You see, Mr. Chang, I was drinking milk through a straw with my friend and the straw slipped into the neckline and suddenly *whoosh*!"

Trick's laughter returned, the boy's face the picture of delight. Then Trick leaned in and kissed him again, the laughter bubbling into his mouth.

Bast took a good taste, finding happiness tasted headier than wine from Trick's lips. "So, wanna get wet? Shower's big enough for two."

"Only two? I'm disappointed." Trick gave him a wink and then backed off, sliding off his jacket and hanging it on the erect penis of a sculpture of a very, *very* happy young man.

Bast chuckled and began the long process of shimmying out of his clothing. "Yeah. Leaves room for things like washing and low-level acrobatics without endangering your partner."

Trick pulled off his t-shirt and his hands moved to his jeans, undoing the button at the top and then stilling. Trick's eyes were on him, filled with heat. "Speaking of acrobatics..."

Bast stopped his gyrating, one arm pulled free of the clinging fabric, one hip bared, skin shining in the low light. "Hmmm?"

Trick blinked slowly, lashes fluttering against his skin. "You need help with that?"

"Oh, yeah. Definitely." Bast shrugged his other shoulder free from the cloth, stomach rolling against the edge of the opened vinyl. The thin line of black curls crowning his cock was just visible, the smell of sex heavy in the air.

Trick stepped closer and slid his hands over Bast's shoulders, fingers sliding in to trace his collarbones, thumbs flicking across his nipples.

"Mmm... your hands are hot." Bast wiggled, partially to free his left arm from the material, but mostly because he liked the random way his body touched Trick's.

Eyes heavy-lidded, Trick continued his silent exploration, leaving a trail of heat wherever he touched. Once or twice, Trick's fingertips slid beneath the vinyl and moved it down an inch or so.

Bast worked his arm free with a soft moan, bending slightly towards Trick as he started working the cloth down his hips, ass swaying and rocking. Trick's hands left him briefly, quickly pushing off his jeans before stepping close again.

Trick's hands cupped Bast's cheeks and tilted his head. Trick's tongue teased and played in his mouth, sweet and rich. Bast's hands stilled, distracted by the taste and feel and smell of the boy before him. Trick's body was close enough to touch, to taste, and Bast teetered on the edge of anticipation.

Then his hands slid over Trick's belly, filling themselves with his warmth. Gasping, Trick pushed against his hands, biting at his lips.

Hot. Oh, by all the dying gods, Trick's skin was so fucking hot. Bast felt a low growl building in his belly, hands sliding up to feel more, to touch the tight nipples.

Trick's hands slid along his skin, getting caught in the vinyl of his suit, fingers fisting through it. "You going to be pissed if I rip this?"

"Only if you don't fuck me through the walls." His nails scratched against Trick's nipples, making the boy hiss. "I want you."

Trick's mouth closed over his again, all teeth and tongue, even as the sound of vinyl splitting accompanied the sudden sensation of air against his naked skin.

Bast pressed against Trick, hands sliding back up into the thick hair, back arching as he let the hot mouth feed on his. Trick grabbed his ass and pulled him up off the floor, tight against the lean body. He wasn't really even aware they were moving until Trick was falling back onto the bed, taking him along. Trick's mouth never left its eager exploration of his.

Undulating against Trick's heat, Bast let his hands play. He teased and explored, finding spot after spot that made Trick arch and moan and cry out into his mouth.

Sheer fucking music.

Trick's fingernails were biting into his ass as Trick pressed him close. Trick was all hard edges, bones and muscles and nails and teeth and erection. Bast explored each edge -- pressing and rubbing and biting as if Trick would slice into his skin and pour his life out onto blazing heat.

At length Trick flipped them over, pressing him into the bed before backing off slightly. "Stuff's in my jeans."

Bast pulled Trick close, one hand reaching for the bedside table and pulling open a drawer and pulled out a condom and a tube of lube. "This work?"

"Like a charm."

Then Trick was kissing him again, and in no time his legs were being pushed open and two hot, slick fingers were sliding slowly into him.

"Oh God, yes. More." Bast arched up with a groan, tongue sliding over Trick's lips, awash in sensation.

Fingers scissoring inside him, Trick bit at his lips. "How do you want it, Bast? Hard, soft, rough, easy, slow, fast -- how do you want me to fuck you?"

"I want to feel you deep, Sweets. Want to feel our bodies together." Bast moaned as Trick's fingers made him arch, hand sliding down the sweat-slick back. "Want to be able to feel you inside me tomorrow."

"I can do that."

Trick's fingers left him empty, but Trick was shifting, moving between his legs, the hot press of Trick's cock tight against him. Trick's eyes met his as the boy slid home.

He would have cried out, but his breath was stolen as his body convulsed, pressure and heat and intensity rocking him. He settled for leaning up and giving Trick a hard, hungry kiss. Trick's mouth clung to his, tongue sliding in as Trick's cock slammed back into his body; it happened over and over again, Trick fucking him hard and deep with tongue and cock.

His orgasm started deep in the back of his skull, electricity shooting along his spine, into his arms and legs. "Oh, fuck! Gonna make me come, Sweets. So hard."

"Oh yeah, babe, come on my cock."

Another kiss, another thrust, and Bast cried out into Trick's mouth, seed spraying between them, body shuddering violently. Thrusts continued to fill him, and then Trick moaned and heat poured into him.

"Mmm... you feel good inside me, Sweets." Bast pressed close, nibbling on Trick's chin and throat. Trick rested on his knees and elbows over Bast, neck arched, exposing himself to the soft touches. "Taste good, too. Rich -- coffee and whiskey and chocolate all rolled into one."

He lapped and nuzzled, purring softly, nipping careful at the skin above the throbbing vein.

"My skin tastes like all that?"

"Oh, yes." Another lick, this one slow and lingering. "Definitely."

Trick chuckled, the sound sated and amused. "Anyone ever tell you you're one strange guy, Bast?"

"I believe that may have been explained to me once or twice, yeah." He smiled against Trick's skin, fingers moving to tickle the boy's unprotected underarms and ribs. Trick giggled, collapsing against Bast as he brought his arms down to try to protect himself from the tickling.

Bast chuckled, wrapping his legs around Trick's waist. He leaned his head back and gave Trick a wicked smile. "Oh, you're ticklish? You're in trouble now, Sweets!"

Trick raised himself up on his elbows, looking at him warily. "You aren't planning on tickling me to death, are you?"

He pretended to consider, admiring the way Trick's skin looked against the dark bedspread. "No. I think we'll have more fun if you're alive and kicking. Besides, it's *such* a challenge to get rid of that dead body smell from the sheets."

Grinning, Trick lowered himself again, wriggling. "Have a lot of experience with that, do you?"

Bast laughed, delighted. "Not for a few centuries, no."

Trick laughed. "A few centuries." He turned his head and nipped sharply at Bast's collarbone. "You crack me up."

"Mm..." Bast let his touch gentle into long, smooth strokes along Trick's flanks. "Good. Laughing is a good thing. Almost as good as moaning."

"As long as they're the right kind of laughing and moaning." There was a tinge of ... *something* in Trick's voice, but then he was nuzzling Bast's neck, lips soft and warm.

Bast arched his neck with a shiver, encouraging the delicious touches. "Yeah, Sweets. Laughing because we're happy and moaning because, oh, it feels good when you do that..."

Trick continued to lick and nibble, tongue sliding over Bast's skin. "Yeah. I forget sometimes, you know?"

"Then I'll have to remind you. You've got a great laugh, Sweets." His hands were moving restlessly, body beginning to respond to Trick's attention.

"You know... you taste like coffee, too. And like that thick red liqueur you get in fancy restaurants." Trick shifted down slightly, tongue and teeth heading for Bast's nipples.

"Oh..." Bast twisted and stretched, a warm pleasure filling him. Relaxed and sated, with need beginning to bubble within him, Bast was surrounded by bliss. Well, he was surrounded by Trick, but it was close enough to be the same and he wasn't about to question his luck.

Trick began to worry Bast's nipples, one between his teeth, the other between surprisingly long fingernails. Bite, pinch and soothe, Trick repeated the pattern over and over.

Soft, hungry moans began to gather in Bast's throat, his body dancing beneath Trick's mouth.

He was the predator, the lover, the one who made his lovers beg and moan and arch. There was something intense and exciting about having Trick's mouth on his body while his was empty, hungry.

"Shit, I forgot what it's like -- to do this because I want to make you moan and come, not because I have to, 'cause you're paying me to." Trick's words were hot against his skin, another caress, hard with honesty.

"Oh, Sweets. Nothing this good should be forgotten." He lifted Trick's chin with a finger and covered the soft, swollen lips with his own, pouring centuries of hunger and skill into burning their shared pleasure into Trick's memory forever.

He could feel Trick trembling against him, the boy's hard cock slick between them as Trick's hips shifted restlessly.

"What do you need, Sweets? I want to hear some of those moans, taste your pleasure on my tongue. What can I do to make you fly?" The words were whispered against Trick's lips, tongue sliding out to taste and touch and keep the burning contact sparking between them.

"Me?" Trick shuddered, a sweet moan sliding against Bast's lips. "You can... you can do anything you want to me."

"You." Bast turned them to their sides, pressing close and letting his mouth work over Trick's skin. His hands slid down to cup Trick's balls, caressing the soft skin for a moment before working the condom off and away from Trick's cock.

The smell of Trick's seed hit him, made him hungry, and he began to lick his way down, tasting nipples and ribs and navel before nipping gently along the line of soft blond curls. Hands slid through his hair, another moan filling the air.

He took his time, learning the texture of each piece of skin with his lips. Trick's cock was hot and smooth, balls soft and tender, inner thighs creamy and addictive -- the rush of life close there, almost as addictive as the music of passion the touch of his teeth drew.

Trick's hands slid away from his hair, twisting in the sheets instead. He pushed up into Bast's mouth. "Oh yeah, baby."

Slowly he licked the come from Trick's cock, long swipes of his tongue alternating with tiny nips and sucks over the silken skin. Then, once the hot flesh was clean and wet, quivering against Trick's belly, he began focusing on the tip, letting himself both pleasure and play.

Trick was whimpering, knuckles white against the blood-red sheets. Bast could feel the boy's muscles trembling with the effort not to push up into his mouth.

"I won't break, Sweets. Let me give you what you want." His hand slid beneath Trick's balls, thumb pushing against the soft skin hidden there. His lips slid over the flared head, nibbling and pulling slightly at the slit, drinking each clear drop as it appeared. "Take what you need, Trick."

A low needy sound passed from between Trick's lips and then his hands were wrapping in Bast's hair, holding him still as Trick began to thrust into his mouth. Trick began slowly, not pushing too deep or too fast or too hard and then all of a sudden, a broken cry sounded and Trick flipped them, fucking his mouth in earnest.

Yes. Oh fuck, yes. Bast took all Trick gave him and demanded more, hands encouraging each thrust, greedy throat swallowing, tongue sliding. His hips were thrusting in time with Trick's, cock throbbing.

"Oh yeah, oh yeah, oh yeah!" Trick shoved hard and came, hips pushing in and out with small, shuddering movements.

It took only the brush of his palm over the head of his own cock and Bast was coming too, body brought to the razor's edge by Trick's passion, Trick's cries, Trick's come sliding down his throat.

Trick pulled out and collapsed next to him, thighs and hips warm, cradling his head. "Fuck, that was good."

"Mm... yeah." Bast nuzzled the soft skin, the smells of sex and musk and Trick surrounding him. "Love how you taste, Sweets. Makes me wild."

Trick's hand slid through his hair and over his face, fingers sliding over his lips, two slipping in. "You're pretty fucking wild without me already."

Bast fastened onto the fingers, sucking gently, eyes falling closed as he relaxed.

Trick moaned softly, hips jerking slightly. "Baby, you're going to kill me."

He let the fingers slip from his lips, slithering up Trick's body and taking a long, soft kiss. "Where's the fun in that?"

Trick curled into him, fingers sliding over his skin in random caresses. It felt good, the heat and touch of Trick's skin, the smell of them on the sheets, Trick's flavor on his tongue. He let one hand trace the curve of Trick's spine, the sleepy kisses becoming softer and more lingering as they relaxed into each other.

"You want me to stay?" The words were spoken with studied casualness; Trick obviously wanted him to think the answer didn't matter one way or another.

"Yes. I want you to stay." Bast's answer was simple, direct, utterly out-of-character, and the complete truth.

Trick sighed, long and deep, and sagged against him, bringing them into contact from nose to toes.

Bast pulled the comforter around them, body being pulled into dreamless rest. He thought about the fact that they should both probably shower, that he should ask if Trick was hungry, that he should say good night or thank you or something.

Instead he moaned softly and snuggled close, sharing Trick's breath, sinking into Trick's rhythm.

Chapter Three

Trick woke up like he always did, eyes open, body alert, fully awake in an instant.

What was unusual was how soft his bed was. And warm. And already occupied. He didn't sleep with his johns and he didn't fuck for pleasure... but he had this time. He had broken all his own rules and gone home with Bast.

And stayed home with Bast.

He couldn't quite bring himself to regret it either; he was warm and relaxed, and he was pretty sure that if he woke Bast up they'd do something about the hard on he was sporting.

Fucking Bast had been like being rolled up in silk, only the feeling lasted long past when the fucking stopped. He was still wrapped in silk: silk sheets, silk skin, even the air seemed soft and gentle.

He could get used to this. And that was the problem.

Bast hadn't moved throughout the night... day... Trick blinked and shook his head. One problem with this underground business is that time never seemed to pass. Everything was lit in blue light.

He looked around for a clock, finding an old fifties-style lime green wind up near the bed. 3 o'clock, then.

He supposed it didn't matter whether it was morning or afternoon, he didn't have anywhere to be; Bast was unlikely to kick him out without feeding him and even if he did, he had a few bucks on him, enough to tide him over until evening when he could go hang out by the alley off Roman.

Sucking cock wasn't exactly something he liked, but it sure beat a lot of the alternatives.

He wondered suddenly what it would be like sucking Bast's cock now. Would it make a difference if he wanted to do it? Would the taste be less bitter if it was his choice?

Curious now, he slid down until his face was buried in Bast's groin. The soft cock began filling almost immediately, the flesh flushed and dark against the pale curve of Bast's hip. Bast stretched out slightly, limbs moving upon the dark sheets, offering more skin to explore.

Trick took his time, exploring the flesh around Bast's cock, nuzzling the dark curls that nested it, nibbling on the sharp hip bones that bracketed it. This wasn't sucking cock, not like he sucked cock for a living; this was exploring, tasting and smelling and feeling the way soft skin gave way to the tickle of hair.

He'd woken up with his own cock hard, and now it was interested, too. Interested in what his mouth was doing, in what his hands were doing to Bast's body.

Bast was moaning for him, more of those interesting, deep moans from the night before that meant yes and please and oh, you make me feel good, Sweets. He mouthed each testicle, pulling them into his mouth, gently sucking and then sliding them around with more force, letting his teeth just barely graze along them as he slid them from his mouth.

Bast's cock he tasted first with his tongue, licking, enjoying the heat and softness of the skin there, taking his time. When he finally took the hard flesh into his mouth, he moaned as he began to suck. Oh, it was like candy, hot and melting on his tongue, and he didn't hope it would be over soon. Not this time -- this time he hoped it would last, last until he'd tasted his full.

"Mm... Sweets. So good." Thin fingers brushed through his hair, leaving his scalp tingling and awake.

Bast rocked slowly, thin body sliding languorously on the sheets, every motion smooth and fluid.

It was good. He slowly sucked Bast all the way in, loving the heat and silk against his tongue, against the roof of his mouth and the back of his throat. He let his fingers slide where they would, one playing with the sharp muscles of Bast's abdomen, the other dancing along the skin behind Bast's balls.

There was nothing jerky or hurried or bitter about this. Bast was clear in his pleasure, letting Trick know with his body, his hands, his husky, rumbling, hungry words, how good and warm and right this felt.

His own hips were rolling against the bed, his heat warming the silk. He continued to suck, humming his own pleasure around the stiff flesh in his mouth.

"Trick, Sweets, I'm close. Real close..." Bast's voice was hoarse, needy as he warned.

He could tell; he'd gotten real good at knowing when someone was about to shoot down his throat and rarely got caught with a mouthful. This time he wanted to taste, wanted Bast's come in his mouth. He sucked harder.

Bast cried out, the sound wild and strange, and then hot seed splashed across his tongue, filling his mouth. The seed was dark and rich, thicker than he expected and almost sweet. The taste of it made him moan and come, soaking the silk he was humping.

"Oh... that makes waking up almost bearable." Bast's hands began moving through his hair again. "Hey, Sweets. How'd you sleep?"

He sucked a moment longer on the sweet flagging flesh and then moved up, pushing Bast over so he didn't have to lie in his wet spot.

"Like the dead. This is one sweet bed."

That apparently amused Bast, who chuckled and wrapped his arms around Trick. "It is."

Bast took a lingering kiss and then settled back, eyes bright. "So are you. Sweet, that is."

He shrugged, not too sure what to make of the compliment, but feeling comfortable enough where he didn't care too much. He didn't get Bast, didn't get what the kid wanted with him, why he wanted him. Didn't trust that this world of soft beds and good, hot fucking would last. 'Course, that was no reason not to enjoy it while it did last, as long as he remembered who and what he was.

He could only get hurt if he came to expect this and more.

Bast's dark eyes were closed again, body still and silent. His breath came, slow and even, almost imperceptible. It was odd, in rest the brightly colored glitterfreak seemed very young, unusually vulnerable.

Trick slid his hand from shoulder to hip, enjoying the feel of Bast's skin, fingers sliding along the bumps and ridges of the tight, wiry muscles. "Everything okay?"

The eyes flared open, almost startled. The lights played tricks with them for a second, making them seem to glow. Then Bast nodded his head and grinned. "You melted my brain. I was trying to decide whether a shower or coffee sounded better. Any preferences?"

Trick considered for a moment and then nuzzled at Bast's neck; he could have coffee anytime. "How big's your shower?"

"Not quite as big as the bed, but close, and I've got three water heaters." Bast chuckled. "I hate cold water."

He rubbed himself against Bast's lithe body. "Then if you think you can get it up again, my vote's for the shower."

"Mm... who's trying to kill who now?" Bast pulled away, sliding off the bed and holding out his hand. "I'm finding you inspirational. Let's get wet."

He let himself be pulled along, eyes widening as they arrived at the bathroom and Bast flicked on the lights. The kid hadn't been kidding about the shower being only slightly smaller than the bed.

Trick flipped the lid on the john, relieving himself as Bast started the water. There was a long counter with bottles of make up and glitter and mousse and hair color, a deep sink, but no mirror.

Glancing around, Trick still couldn't find any glass, and he wondered how Bast managed to apply all the pretty stuff without one. Maybe it was hidden and there was a button you pressed that flipped a part of the wall like in some James Bond movie. The thought had him chuckling as he joined Bast beneath the hot spray.

Two shower heads worked to splash hot water liberally upon the black stone, Bast stretching along one wall as the jets pounded against his skin. Dark eyes welcomed him. "What's funny?"

Trick felt his cock come back to life, growing heavy between his legs, and he pressed up against Bast, rubbing himself on the slick body. "I was just looking for the button."

"Button?" One of Bast's legs curled around his hip, sliding over his ass. The room was filling with steam, blurring the contrast between pale skin and dark marble. He could feel Bast's cock against him, hotter than the water.

"Yeah..." he moaned and put his mouth on Bast's neck, sucking the water noisily from the fine skin. "The one that turns this room into a real bathroom."

"Oh, that's good, so good." Bast's head fell back as he arched. "I keep the real bathroom in the batcave, Sweets."

Trick chuckled, but most of his attention was on the way Bast's skin moved beneath his mouth, the way it flavored the water he sucked in, making it something exotic. The long line of Bast's neck begged to be loved, and he nibbled his way from shoulder to jaw and back down again before settling on a spot just above where Bast's shoulder met his neck and beginning to suck. His hands slid down and cupped Bast's ass, pulling them tightly together as he thrust with his hips, wishing he were buried deep inside the silky hot body.

Bast came alive beneath Trick's mouth and hands, low hungry growls echoing beneath the water. Undulations became something more feral, less fluid. The steam mixed with the cool marble and the burning body in his hands, becoming something unbearably erotic.

He bit down hard as he came, his scream silent.

Bast was limp and sated in his arms when his brain coalesced, mouth working against his shoulder, water still pounding hot against them.

He slid slowly to the ground, taking Bast with him, shuddering as their skin moved together.

He was panting, exhausted, but in a wonderful, boneless and totally sated way. He couldn't remember ever feeling this good inside his own body.

A husky whisper was barely audible over the water. "I should look into having a mattress installed in here. We're never gonna make it back to the bed."

"It's not part of the batcave version?" He giggled at his own joke, sobering slowly. "You're right though -- I don't think I can move. I may never move again."

Bast chuckled as Trick's stomach rumbled loudly. "Oh, I don't know. There's pecan pie and a warm bed and coffee out there, Sweets. I bet you'll move eventually."

"Eventually being the operative word."

He settled against the tiles next to Bast, one hand wrapped possessively around Bast's hip. Bast's head fit nicely against his shoulder, the long black hair covering much of Bast's skin. Trick shook his head as the soft lips brushed against his throat. No false words of adoration, no coldness, nothing but warm hunger and appreciation and something nearing affection came from Bast. It was as unnerving as it was satisfying.

"I could wash you, if you wanted."

"Oh...sounds like heaven, Sweets." A pale hand reached up and returned with a small chunk of dark brown soap, and suddenly one of the elements of the fascinating smell that was Bast clicked into place.

He moved to kneel between Bast's legs, rubbing up a lather on his hands, the scent of patchouli and sandalwood strong, like the inside of one of those witchy stores, all incense and old books. It shouldn't have suited Bast, but it did.

His hands were slick on Bast's skin, sliding over the places he'd caressed and kissed. He pressed the mark he'd left on Bast's neck, wondering if it was as sensitive as it looked.

A soft growl and Bast arched, cock visibly trying to respond, twitching as it swelled. "Oh, fuck, Sweets. You're going to kill me."

"You like that?" It wasn't really a question, and he pressed again, fingers sliding past the mark again and again as he washed Bast with his other hand.

He covered every inch of skin and then came back to do Bast's cock last.

It made him feel good, to give this pleasure, to offer it freely. It made him want to push the boundaries, push Bast; could he make the man come again?

Bast's dark eyes were closed, body arched and stretched beneath Trick. Shivers passed beneath the skin, the steam and water making him almost seem to glow. "Oh, fuck. You feel so good. You make me feel so fucking good."

He watched, his own body fighting its way to arousal, his cock half hard already as Bast responded to his touch. He wrapped his soap-slicked hand around Bast's erection, stroking him. A low keening filled the hair, Bast's legs splaying wide, hips moving toward the touches.

"Fucking shit, you're incredible." He squeezed tighter, moved his hand faster, dropping into the rhythm he liked best himself. He pressed down hard on his mark on Bast's neck with his thumb, letting his fingernail press into the skin.

Bast's body convulsed, his eyes flying open, his cock throbbing as thick seed pulsed over Trick's hand. The steam seemed to change the dark eyes for a second, before the heavy lids fell again, Bast almost sobbing in reaction.

Trick let the water sluice over Bast for a moment, washing away seed and soap alike, and then he bent and laid a kiss on Bast's belly and another on his lips. "You're like some magic creature and I keep waiting to wake up and find out this has all been a dream."

"Not a dream. Swear it." Bast lips moved clumsily, words slurred, limbs completely limp.

Trick let his hand slide down the smooth body once more. "Yeah, you feel pretty real."

He licked the water from Bast's lips and then slid his tongue between them for another long kiss. Then he stood and turned the shower off, the room suddenly silent with the water no longer pounding at the tiles and their skin. The towels were easy to find, hanging on a rack that warmed them, and he shook his head as he took one and wrapped Bast in it; it must be nice to have money to burn.

He picked Bast up, grunting slightly at the effort and, dripping himself, carried Bast over to the divan.

"I don't know about you, but I'm starving and pecan pie ain't gonna do it. Do they deliver down here?"

"They do. Phone's in the big cabinet." Bast pointed to the series of ornate cabinets that took up at least eight feet along the wall. There was a leather desk chair sitting before it. "Any place close by, just tell 'im Sebastian Apostolos' place, under the mural building. They'll find me."

The cabinet was full of drawers and doors. In pulling them open he found Bast's computer, television, stereo, DVD player, security system, dozens of pieces of electronic equipment he didn't even recognize and then, finally, the perfectly normal, plain, white telephone sitting atop a yellow pages.

"What do you feel like? I could eat a horse." He grinned a little self-consciously. "All that sex..."

"Mm... I'm not a big eater, Sweets. I have a liquid diet mostly. Coffee, protein shakes, that sort." The dark eyes cracked open. "Tony's delivers here. They make one hell of a sliced beef sandwich. Or there's a pizza joint on the corner, nice little lady runs it."

"I don't think a sandwich is going to cut it -- not if I'm staying past eating." He grabbed the phonebook, blindly flipping through it as he glanced covertly at Bast, waiting for his response.

Bast nodded, then his eyes fluttered open and his head tilted. "Hey, there's an all-night grocery that delivers. They make fried chicken and barbecue and these wicked fruit shakes. We could get enough to tide us through a few more showers. I seem to remember a monster movie festival on HBO tonight, if you're interested."

Relief flooded through him and that worried him a little, but he pushed it away -- there was nothing wrong with checking out for a while. Bast was sexy and fun and rich and gave incredible head. "Sounds good. Food, sex, and monsters, what else could I ask for?"

"Long, hot showers." Bast grinned over. "Let's make a list and then I'll make the call -- unless you speak Greek?"

Trick laughed. "No, but you do? Is that where you're from? Greece?" He picked up a pad of paper and a pen and went back to the divan, sitting close to Bast, sitting almost on top of him; he loved the feel of Bast's skin against his own.

"That's where I was born, yeah. Haven't been back in ages." Bast curled close, eyes dropping closed. "But I can still speak the language enough to get by."

He smoothed through the raven hair for a moment, chuckling when his stomach growled. "That settles it -- food, now."

"Chicken or barbeque or both?" Bast grinned. "Go grab the pie to tide you over, growly."

"Both -- who knows, you may decide you're hungry after your next orgasm, or ten." He looked around, finding the pie on a table near the elevator. Grabbing it, he headed back toward the divan wolfing it down as he went.

Bast was standing, stark naked, chattering away into the phone, hands waving exaggeratedly. He grinned over at Trick, rolling his eyes and gathering up the remote control and throwing it on the bed.

Trick could get used to this, to this easy, lazy lifestyle where all that mattered was if you had enough food and entertainment to last between bouts of awesome sex.

He could get used to wandering up to Bast, standing behind the man and cradling his growing erection in the small of Bast's back, one arm around the wiry chest. For now though he'd just enjoy it, take every sensation that Bast had to offer and revel in it and when Bast booted him out the door, a day or two down the line... well, he'd have a few memories to keep his hand company.

Bast nestled back against him, a quick kiss given to the bottom of his chin in between sentences. Finally the phone was set down and Bast grinned, turning to face him. "Half an hour and we'll be stocked up. How was the pie?"

"Saved you a corner." He held the bit up to Bast's lips.

Bast shook his head, licking at Trick's fingers with a quick pink tongue. "Too sweet and I'm nowhere near as hungry as you are."

He shrugged and it slid their skin together. "Your loss -- it's damn good pie." He slipped the piece into his mouth, exaggerating his pleasure.

Dark eyes grinned at him, suddenly warm again. "I swear, watching you eat... if I hadn't come eighteen times in the last twelve hours, I'd tackle you, Sweets."

"Eighteen times?" Trick laughed. "Oh, I'm good, but I'm not that good."

Bast's laughter joined his and then he was given a quick kiss before Bast danced away, flopping down onto the bed. "Come on, let's watch movies. You can hold my hand when I get scared."

He moved more slowly, eyes on Bast as he made his way to the bed. "I used to get scared watching these when I was little."

"Then I'll hold your hand, too." Bast turned, giving Trick a lovely view of back and legs and sweetly curved ass, black hair falling damp and wavy around him.

"I'm not scared anymore." Not since one of his mother's boyfriends had sat him down and cut open his hand, making him compare the blood on the television to the blood on his hand. "They're just make believe. Ketchup and paint and moody music."

He slipped onto the bed and spooned up against Bast.

"You think they use ketchup? Funky!" Bast grimaced and clicked on the television, flipping through channels and playing with the volume until he was satisfied. Little green monsters that lived in the sewer appeared, the cheesy dialogue and terrible special effects making Bast chuckle.

Trick only half paid attention to the television, preferring to shift Bast's hair and nibble on his neck and run his fingers over the muscled abdomen, learning Bast's skin. Bast was sleek and smooth -- no scars, no moles, hardly any hair except for the thick mass on his head and the curls above his cock.

His own cock had responded to their proximity and was nestled against Bast's buttocks, and when he let his hand slide down past the curls, he discovered that Bast's cock was hard and eager for his touch.

Bast met his eyes sheepishly. "You're inspiring."

Leaning over Bast, he brought their lips together for a long kiss as he stroked the hard flesh in his hand. Sweet and open, Bast's lips were addictive as they moved with his own, tongue flicking out to taste.

"You make me hungry, Sweets. Hungry and hot."

"Then I guess you'd better eat." He murmured the words against Bast's mouth, tongue and teeth keeping contact with the kiss-reddened lips.

Bast gave an odd, needy cry, body pushing close, eyes dropping closed. The thin cheeks flushed, becoming heated and red. "Oh, Sweets. You're temptation incarnate."

Trick chuckled, moving his hips, letting his cock slide along Bast's buttocks, his hand continuing to pump Bast's erection. "I thought you'd already given in to temptation, not quite eighteen times."

"In twelve hours... don't forget that part." Bast was panting lightly, hips rocking. "That's the impressive part."

"Yes, very impressive," Trick agreed, going back to nibbling on the tempting neck. He couldn't see the mark he'd left -- Bast was lying on that side -- but he supposed he could add a match for it. He began to scrape the skin with his teeth.

Bast turned, face burying in the curve of Trick's throat. "Oh, no. My turn to taste. I need to taste you, Sweets."

Trick moaned as their erections met, hot and hard together. No marks. It was another rule he had with his johns. He opened his mouth to protest and realized that he wanted Bast to mark him. "Yes," he breathed, hands moving to explore the length of Bast's spine.

Lips fastened onto his throat, Bast's teeth sharp against his skin. A flare of bright pain as Bast bit down and then the bottom fell out from beneath Trick. A wave of pleasure hit him, washing over him like the first night he'd been inside Bast.

He screamed his pleasure, hips jerking as he came hot and hard with barely any stimulation.

He floated for a minute, ten minutes, an hour -- he wasn't sure, but when he opened his eyes, his arms where full of a limp and gently purring Bast, tongue moving over his skin in intricate patterns.

"Wow... What the fuck was that?"

Maybe the sugar from the pie had hit him just at the right time, or maybe Hannah's secret was some wild aphrodisiac and that's what kept people coming back.

"Ah, you see, I'm a vampire and it feels really wicked cool when I feed from you." The phrase was delivered in a completely dry tone, Bast's eyes shining up at him.

Trick laughed and rolled over top of Bast, nipping at the mark he'd left. "I'm Count Dracula and I've come to suck your blood." He said the words in his most silly Transylvanian accent, the fact that a close approximation to the same words were spoken on the television tickling him all the more. "Who needs HBO -- we can make our own home horror movies."

"You get the ketchup, I'll find some moody music." Bast was giggling in his arms, fingers ineffectually trying to tickle him.

"I've got an even better idea -- lets skip the ketchup and the music and just do the sucking part." He closed his teeth over Bast's skin and then soothed the bite with his tongue. "After we've eaten -- that last one really wiped me out."

"Mm... I vaguely remember hearing a buzzer when we were busy earlier. I'll run up and see if the food's here." Bast kissed him on the nose. "You see if the next movie's any good."

Trick watched Bast go, admiring the sexy sway of hips and the way Bast's hair swung over his back. He lay back on the bed, idly watching the next movie start, not really paying attention to it. Even though he didn't think he could move, he felt good. He hadn't felt this good in a long time.

The rattles and groans from the elevator filled the apartment, then stopped for a moment and then started again, this time accompanied by a low voice singing something odd and foreign.

Bast was such an odd guy; he seemed so young and so old at the same time. He was unbelievably fantastic in bed. He seemed to have no responsibilities and was loaded.

Trick couldn't decide if he wanted to be Bast or just get fucked by him for the rest of his life. He shook his head and focused on the movie; he knew better than to ask for things that were out of his reach.

The gate opened and Bast dragged in a box full of bags and boxes and bottles. "Look what I found, Sweets. Enough supplies to last at least six orgasms."

Trick chuckled and eyed the groceries. "Look more like enough to last six days. Want a hand?"

"Yeah." Bast was grinning as he pulled the cardboard across the room, pushing open a thin door that led into what Trick figured was the kitchen. "Tell you what, I'll put the stuff away, you hand it in to me?"

Trick dragged himself up and began to rustle through the box. "Oh, the fried chicken smells amazing." He put the small box aside and flashed Bast a grin. "See, I'm saving you work already."

Bast cackled, pushing his dark hair over his shoulder as he stacked items throughout the surprisingly tiny kitchen. "Such a help you are."

"I'm guessing you're not much of a cook," Trick noted as he continued to hand over the groceries. He snagged a Coke to go with his chicken.

"Uh, no. Not really. I'm kind of a... simple eater. Macrobiotics and stuff. Lots of protein drinks."

Trendy, Trick thought. It fit with the skin-tight cat suits and the clubbing, but not with the old-fashioned sounding ballad and the Greek. Bast was like his home; a study in contradictions that all seemed to work well together.

Bast finished throwing things into cabinets and then grabbed a bottle of water from the fridge and the aluminum-wrapped package of barbecued meat from the counter. "Here's the rest of dinner, Sweets. You find a good movie?"

"I wasn't really paying attention," he admitted sheepishly. No, he'd been enjoying the afterglow, but that was something he wasn't going to admit.

"Mm... post-sex floaties. Those are the best." Bast leaned up, took a quick, playful kiss and bounced back onto the bed, full of energy.

Trick followed more slowly and sat cross-legged on the bed, opening the carton of fried chicken and digging in. His stomach growled in appreciation.

Bast grinned, sipping at his water and curling around Trick's back. His body pressed close as he grabbed the remote. "Ah... 'The Hunger' -- David Bowie makes a sexy vampire, even if he's a bit crazy."

"His eyes are freaky -- and did you know he used to wear dresses? Face is too odd to be a pretty girl though." Trick licked spices and grease from his fingers. "This is really good chicken."

"Dresses, huh? Takes a special kind of guy to wear those. I can pull off the hair and the walk, but I'm too thin, all hips and angles." Bast's thin hand tickled over his belly. "You, now you'd never make it as a chick. Your walk is all balls."

"What's that supposed to mean?"

"You don't walk like a girl. You walk like a hunter. No one would ever mistake you for a chick."

"And you like that, don't you?" He wriggled his ass back into Bast's groin.

"Fuck, yes." Fingers found his nipples, began to twist and tweak. "Your walk is pure sex appeal, Sweets. Like dancing."

"Fucking. Dancing is like fucking." He gasped and arched, cock stirring, what was left of the chicken forgotten.

"Mm... yeah." Bast slithered over to straddle Trick's lap, body undulating to the throbbing music coming from the television. "Dancing with you is a dream."

He slid his arms around to Bast's back, hands moving down to cup Bast's ass, pulling their groins closer together. Slim hands wrapped around his neck, ebony eyes bright on his face. Bast rocked and danced, muscles rippling, skin soft and silky.

Trick moaned as Bast rubbed against him, fingers sliding across his lover's opening, teasing the wrinkled flesh.

"Mm..." With a shiver and a sweet groan, Bast pushed up on his knees, hair falling all around Trick, slick and cool. "Tease."

He just grinned and leaned forward, tongue sliding over Bast's skin, fingers sliding down to cup the heavy balls and tickle the flesh between Bast's thighs.

Bast arched into him, crying out. "Trying to kill me. Only so many orgasms one guy can have a day, Sweets."

"What's your best day?"

"Oh, fuck, Sweets... I... six, maybe seven. Comes a point where you're just one bundle of nerves and sorta lose track."

"So we're going for eight then." Trick grinned and began to nibble on Bast's nipples, playing first one and then the other in quick succession.

"Going for..." Bast's body shifted, twisting as if he couldn't decide whether to ask for more or beg Trick to stop. "You are trying to kill me."

Trick leaned back, hands on the bed behind him. "I could leave if you want. Of course then you'd always wonder if I could do it. If I could make you come more in one day than you ever have before."

Bast looked at him. "I don't want you to go, Sweets. You make me fly."

Trick grinned. "Good."

He reached up and slid his finger across one of Bast's nipples, letting his nail drag across it as well. Bast hissed, head falling backward, hair pooling on the mattress.

He pinched the other nipple, and then raked his nails across Bast's stretched out stomach. His lover arched farther, body bowlike and graceful, pink marks showing on the flat stomach for a few heartbeats before fading.

He scratched again across Bast's belly and then along one inner thigh, fascinated by the way the pale skin seemed to absorb the marks he made. Stomach muscles rippled as Bast pulled himself up with nothing more than his own strength, cheeks flushed and eyes bright and hungry.

Watching Bast's face he scrapped his nails over the hot, silky cock.

Bast convulsed with a soft cry, eyes widening as shudders moved through him. "Fuck..."

"You like that?" He did it again.

Another cry sounded and Bast was coming, heat splashing over his hand. Trick surged up and took Bast's mouth, hot and hungry from watching his lover's pleasure, from causing it. Bast made him feel hot and sexy and powerful. It was becoming addictive, the rush he got from making Bast come.

Bast met his kiss with a groan of hunger, hands flying up to tangle in his hair, body pushing, hot and damp, against his cock.

"What do you want, Bast? You want more? You want me to come in you or on you?"

Bast's lips moved to his ear, nibbling as he whispered. "Want you to fuck me again. Love the feel of your cock inside me, Sweets."

Oh, yeah, this man was addictive, and Trick didn't even care anymore. He dove in, tongue plunging into Bast's mouth, even as he pressed a finger into Bast's body. Bast pushed down against Trick's hand, sucking on Trick's tongue as the lean body rode him, movements fierce and needy.

Bast was ready, Trick was ready; he wouldn't make either of them wait. His hand wasn't quite steady as he pulled open the drawer where Bast kept his condoms and he had to use his teeth to rip the packet open, but it didn't take too long before he was pushing into Bast.

"Oh, yeah. Good... it's so good." Bast tilted his hips, grabbing his legs and holding himself open for Trick's cock, touch, eyes.

He sank in deep and then began to thrust immediately, fast and hard, falling into Bast and the sensations they created together. Bast met each stroke, arching and writhing beneath him. Hot and welcoming and so responsive, Bast held nothing back, feeding his joy and pleasure back to Trick with every cry and moan.

Trick was out of control, fucking Bast wildly, just pushing in and pulling out and feeling so fucking good. So good that he was screaming, cock buried deep inside Bast as he came.

Warm arms and legs wrapped around him, held him close, lips periodically tasting his skin, his mouth. Bast rested, relaxed and quiet with him.

He felt so good. All glowy, tired but in a happy, floating kind of way. He didn't have to indulge in post-sex kitten talk, he didn't have the urge to grab his money and get out of there as quickly as possible; he just felt. Oh, this was going to be hard to let go of.

Even that knowledge couldn't impinge on the experience; that was later, maybe a few days, maybe a few hours or even just minutes, but later. For now he gave himself permission to just enjoy what was at this moment in his hands.

A blanket drifted over his shoulders, the touch soft and silken and warm. Bast just continued his gentle nuzzling and touching, encouraging Trick to relax, the television a quiet murmur in the background.

He was warm and sated and safe, and while he didn't trust it, he liked it. He settled heavily against Bast and let himself drift.

Chapter Four

Bast worked quietly and efficiently, debugging the odd line of code in his latest project, answering emails and questions, fingers moving over the keyboard in an odd one-handed method born from years of typing on the laptop while lounging in bed.

Periodically he would stretch, smiling as his skin slid along Trick's.

The boy was something else -- a fascinating mixture of cold and hot. So passionate and hungry and angry -- and yet there was a vulnerability that rested beneath all that.

Bast sighed, uploading some changes onto the server. These humans were all vulnerable. It was the nature of the animal.

Trick moved, wrapping one arm around his waist and nuzzling against his back. Bast found himself impossibly growing hard again, pushing into the touch. Vulnerable, perhaps, but Trick made him burn inside, made him ache.

"'ve I been 'sleep long?"

"Mmm... a few hours, I think. You looked warm and happy, so I just let you sleep." Bast shut the laptop and set it on the bedside table before turning in Trick's arms, snuggling close. "Hey, Sweets. Have good dreams?"

"Yeah." Trick's mouth closed over his, the kiss slick and slow. "I dreamt I was in a soft bed made of silk with a man who was a monster in bed."

Bast chuckled. "Sounds delicious. Good thing I'm only a monster when I'm up and dressed, otherwise you wouldn't know if you were awake." He trailed his hand down Trick's spine in a slow caress, appreciating the smooth, warm skin.

Trick chuckled, and his hand slid down to circle Bast's hard cock. "Oh, I think you're a monster in bed, too, but I'm not complaining. If I'm still dreaming, don't wake me."

"Oh, it's a deal." Bast pushed up into Trick's hand, murmuring against Trick's lips. "I can't be hard again. My balls have got to be empty. So, this has to be a dream."

"Then let's never wake up." Trick's mouth closed over his, tongue thrusting rhythmically, matching the long strokes over his erection. Trick's own heat was hard and slick against his belly.

Bast let himself wrap around Trick, his body and hands almost dancing against his lover. He shouldn't be so hungry, shouldn't be so needy -- but he was and it was good and Bast was nothing if not skilled at losing himself to sensation.

Trick fed from his lips as if they hadn't spent the last day wrapped in each other's arms, sating their hunger over and over again. Trick acted as if he were starving, as if he only had this one chance to fill the hole inside him with what he craved.

That was something Bast understood in the marrow of his bones -- hunger. Bast responded, answering that hunger with passion and desire, giving Trick everything he asked for and beyond that, some of what he needed.

Something inside the boy responded to that, eased and for the first time Trick asked for what he wanted. "Want you to fuck me." The request was softly spoken, tentative, as if Trick would pull it back and deny it at the slightest provocation, but it was asked nonetheless.

"Anything you want, Sweets." Bast continued the drugging kisses, continued touching the warm skin, even as he coated his fingers in lube. He began by sliding his fingers over Trick's cock, circling the soft, heavy sacs.

Then, when Trick was arching and moaning against him, he let his fingers wander back behind Trick's balls, stroking the delicate, hidden skin.

Trick whimpered, trembling in his arms. "Bast..."

"Yeah, Sweets? Does it feel good?" Bast let his fingers travel further back, working to find every ounce of sensation, of pleasure for his lover.

Trick answered not with words but with his body, dancing between the sensations Bast showered over him. Trick's kisses were sloppy, hungry, becoming almost harsh as Bast slid his fingers deep inside Trick's body. Tight and hot, heartbeat pulsing around his fingers, the pressure made Bast ache, made him want to bury himself inside that silken heat. More than that, he wanted Trick to know want, hunger, and blessed satiation at his hands.

Trick moved between sensations, pushing back onto his fingers and then pushing into his body, into the kisses they shared.

Bast pushed deeper, finding the smooth gland with his fingers and stroking over it, capturing Trick's cry with his mouth.

One of Trick's hands wrapped around his hip, the other around his shoulder, fingernails digging in as Trick clung to him, body trembling and shuddering and begging for more.

"Are you ready for me, Sweets? Ready to let me in?" Bast whispered the words against Trick's lips, reaching for a condom even as his fingers moved over the hidden gland keeping Trick awash in pleasure.

"Yes." Trick's whisper was desperate, needy.

Bast rolled the condom on, slicking himself generously and then moving between Trick's legs. His fingers pressed and stroked until Trick was twisting and sobbing, then, with an ease that was like breathing, Bast slid his fingers out and his cock into perfect heat.

Trick's cry was choked off as the boy bit into Bast's shoulder, but not even that could hide the needy whimpers or the way Trick writhed on his cock, trying to impale himself further.

"Yes, lovely. I want you, too." Bast began to rock, whimpering at the feel of Trick all around him. "Feels so good, Trick. So sweet."

Trick's face was buried in his neck, lips and teeth grazing his skin. "Please, oh, please." The soft words were mouthed more than spoken.

"Yes. Anything you need, Sweets. Anything you need." The words slipped from his lips as his hips pressed deep, body arching into Trick.

"More." Trick demanded.

"Oh, yes." Bast pulled back, letting his hips snap back into Trick's body, the threat of feral hunger awakening at the base of his spine.

Trick screamed, back arching, and then spoke again, the single word still a command, a demand and a plea. "More."

A low growl left him and everything went bright and sharp, pleasure becoming almost unbearable. He fought the hunger fiercely, even as his body responded to Trick's need, thrusting harder and deeper. Trick was sobbing with each thrust, screaming out the word again and again and again, hands clinging.

Bast took Trick's lips, taking a fierce, harsh kiss, the taste of blood hot and sweet as Trick's lip caught against his teeth. He pulled Trick against him, slamming them together, Trick's cock a brand against his stomach. Trick's screams and whimpers filled his mouth along with the drops of blood. The boy's writhing had become desperate. One hand circled Trick's cock and Bast drank Trick in -- hunger, blood, need, desire -- all of it. He fed on it, letting Trick's flavor sink into his bones, deep inside him.

Trick froze, body impossibly tight and still and then he was shuddering, come pouring from him.

"Yes!" Trick's pleasure tasted so good, so fucking good and his body was tight and close and right and the lights seemed to dim when Bast came, jerking against Trick's body. "Fuck, yes."

Trick lay heavy against him, body warm and lax around him. Trick's eyes were closed, his breath coming in harsh gasps, chest rising and falling, sweat-slicked and glowing in the blue light.

Bast relaxed, pulling out of the sweet heat with a moan. He reached for the bottle of water on the little table, dropping it twice before he managed to make it to his mouth. He placed the tip to Trick's lips. "Want a drink, Sweets? Cold water?"

Moaning, Trick opened glazed eyes, blinking at him. Finally nodding, Trick's mouth opened and he cupped the bottle, swallowing when Bast tilted it.

Bast closed the cap, let it fall from the side of the bed and he curled around Trick, body heavy with warmth and exhaustion. "You're amazing."

Trick burrowed into him. "Gonna die happy, anyway."

"Mm... hell of a plan, that." Bast stroked the damp blond hair, fingers lazy and slow. His body was exhausted but tingling with pleasure.

"I don't think I can move." Trick informed him. "I don't know if I'll ever be able to move again."

"No problem. The remotes are close and there's water. Hell, the laptop's right here. We can send out for someone to wash sheets and bring coffee in a week or two." Bast grinned, chuckling low and warm. "Assuming, of course, that I put my brain together enough to remember how to log on." Although these *were* the moments where a manservant would come in handy.

"I didn't know... sex could be like that. Good like that, I mean." Trick buried his face back into Bast's neck and he could feel the heat of Trick's flushed cheeks.

"It was amazing." Bast nuzzled Trick with his chin. "You're amazing, Sweets. We were amazing together. Maybe once we've recovered, we can see if the first twenty amazing orgasms were just a fluke."

"You're going to need to order more food. Or I'm never going to get it up again."

"I can do that. As soon as I get enough energy to raise my head. I mean, really, we've got "Pee Wee's Big Adventure" on the television and I can't reach the remote. Even I have priorities."

Trick snorted. "I think Pee Wee's already had his big adventure."

Bast laughed merrily, finding the energy to grab a pillow and smack Trick's butt with it. "That was absolutely terrible."

"Well I'm not here for my stand-up routine." Trick paused a moment and then added, "Or maybe I am," before giggling madly.

"Oh, that's it." Bast rolled on the bed, holding his stomach as he cackled, grabbing another pillow. "Prepare to defend yourself, foul fiend!"

Trick tried to grab the pillow above him and roll out of the way of the one Bast launched at him and wound up ass first on the floor.

Bast leaned over, peering down at Trick with a grin. "Uh, Trick? The bed's big, but not that big."

Trick blinked up at him for a moment. "I thought size wasn't supposed to matter." Trick's lips turned up into a grin and then he began to laugh, curling up around himself, shoulders shaking.

The nice thing about sleeping with a lot of pillows was that you didn't run out of ammunition quickly, Bast decided, as he pelted Trick from his position on the mattress.

He was laughing so hard he hurt, tears sliding down his face. Happiness rolled through him as he played with his friend, played and laughed, and it felt so good hearing that laugh.

So good. As good as -- even better than -- the sex.

Trick finally uncurled and sat, wiping away his own tears of mirth. "So can we count that as number eight, 'cause I swear it felt as good as the sex."

"Eight? Hell, number twenty-four!" Bast held out his hand. "Come on, you nut. Get back up here and keep me warm. Bugs Bunny will be on soon."

Trick grabbed his hand and pulled himself up, but headed away from the bed, scratching his stomach. "Gotta use the facilities first."

Bast nodded, admiring the fine lines of his ass. "Want some food? Coffee?"

"Yeah, I'll raid your kitchen in a sec." Trick disappeared into the bathroom.

Bast got out of bed, wandering into the kitchen. His refrigerator looked odd full of food and he shook his head. At some point Trick was going to question his eating habits. Hopefully the truth wouldn't ruin everything.

He heard the toilet flush and then the soft slap of Trick's feet against the floor. A warm arm wound around his shoulder, Trick's body warm against his back as the boy leaned on him. "So what looks good?"

"You mean besides you?" Bast teased gently. "There's eggs and oatmeal and bacon. Lots of fruit. And barbecue."

"You got any ice cream and a blender? We could throw in the fruit and some ice -- have smoothies. Besides," Trick bumped his hips against Bast's ass. "You're the one who looks good, but I already ate you."

Bast nodded, rolling his eyes and snuggling back against Trick. "Smoothies work, funny boy. I've got strawberries, pineapple, peaches, and some cherries. What's your pleasure?"

"You gonna beat me with a pillow again if I mention how I can't believe you have any cherries left?"

"Yeah. Yeah, I probably will." Bast lifted his chin and took a quick kiss, enjoying the flavors of laughter. "You'll notice I didn't mention the bananas?"

"You got bananas and strawberries?" Trick's eyes had lit up. "They work great together. When I was real little my mom used to make banana splits with strawberry ice cream every payday. Best combination ever."

"Really? Cool!" Bast chuckled and started pulling out fruits and ice and a container of vanilla ice cream. "I think I'll have pineapple and orange juice, nice and tart."

He'd make himself a drink without the cream -- the juice would taste good going down and stay, but the milk wouldn't settle, and he didn't think Trick was quite ready for his particular dietary needs.

Trick snickered and Bast could almost hear him debating whether or not to say anything. "Nice and tart -- like you, right?"

Bast gave Trick his best wide-eyed and innocent look. "As opposed to sweet and creamy -- like you?"

Trick laughed at that, eyes crinkling, mouth smiling widely, and suddenly Trick turned him and pushed him up against the marble counter, kissing him. Bast twined his arms around Trick's neck, returning the kiss happily. The feel of Trick's skin against his was addictive.

"I thought you were hungry."

"I am -- starving." He kissed Bast again, long and slow, hips circling, rubbing their cocks together, encouraging them to grow. "This suddenly seemed more important."

"Mm..." Bast reached out and rubbed a strawberry along Trick's bottom lip. "Got to keep your strength up."

Once Trick nibbled up the strawberry, Bast opened a banana, feeding it to his lover between long, fruity kisses.

"Mom's strawberry banana splits never tasted this good," Trick whispered, licking Bast's fingers clean.

"Mm... I'm honored." Bast nibbled on Trick's shoulder, enjoying the sweet-salt flavor.

Then he picked up a cherry and rubbed it on Trick's nipple, bending to lap the sweetness off.

"Oh, yeah, you've got my cherry all right." Trick chuckled and moaned at the same time, cock jerking against Bast's skin.

Bast groaned and nipped sharply at the skin beneath his teeth. "I'll show you *cherry*, Sweets."

The utter idiocy of his own comment made him giggle, laughing happily on Trick's skin. Trick's nipples were hard beneath his lips, laughter punctuated by soft moans and gasps.

Bast sank to his knees, licking along the warm, jumping stomach, before nibbling along the line of gold curls that crowned the full cock. "Mm...sweet."

"Bast... oh..." Trick's fingers slid through his hair, tugging him toward the hard flesh.

Bast opened his lips, tongue flicking out to taste and tease. The first night, in the club, it had been quick and easy. Now he could play, taste and lick and suck and tease and enjoy the flavor of Trick's body.

Trick took a long, shaky breath and his hands fisted into Bast's hair.

With the skill of his years, Bast made love to Trick with his mouth. They'd played, they'd fucked, they'd fed in one way or another from each other. This was different, slow and easy and, at least in Bast's mind, warm and good.

Trick's hands left his hair and planted themselves on the counter, his legs spreading as tiny whimpers sounded.

"Bast..." His name was spoken softly, full of need and want and something close to joy.

Bast hummed softly, hands moving to stroke the soft inner thighs, feel the steady beat of Trick's heart. He took Trick deep, letting him slip inside his throat for a few heartbeats, and then backed away, repeating the rhythm again and again.

"Gonna come," Trick whispered, soft and low like he was worried he was going to break the spell cast around them, the one that held them within pleasure's grasp.

Bast let his throat relax, slid his lips to the base of Trick's cock and sucked, fingers moving up to entwine with Trick's, holding them together.

"Bast!" Trick came, come pouring down his throat, hips jerking.

He sucked gently, enjoying each tremor, each fading sign of pleasure. Then, when Trick was clean and soft in his mouth, he let his lover slip free and nuzzled against the warm belly.

One of Trick's hands stayed tangled with his, the other slid through his hair, softly, over and over.

"Mm..." Bast closed his eyes, resting happily, the taste of passion burning on his tongue, the sound of Trick's heartbeat in his head. Trick slid down to his own knees and searched blindly for his mouth, lips clinging, breath soft and fruity.

The kiss lasted until the tang of fruit and the salt of Trick's seed was gone and all that was left was the joint flavor of their mouths and tongues.

Trick rested his forehead against Bast's, eyes closed, mouth open as he panted. Twice Bast felt him tense, jaw dropping to say something, and twice Trick remained silent.

Bast rubbed his cheek against Trick's. "You all right, Sweets?"

The blue eyes opened, met his. He read satiation in them, deep and mixed in with happiness, and stark, honest hunger. "I'm scared," Trick whispered, the words costing him a shudder, and his lids fell, hiding his eyes and the secrets they gave away.

Bast kissed Trick's forehead, searching for the right words. He finally settled with a promise he could keep. "I won't ask anything from you that you don't want to share, Sweets. You have my word."

Trick shook his head, but didn't say anything else, just lay against him, body still and warm. He held Trick, hand stroking against the thick hair, until long after his legs had gone numb and his heat had been leached away into the tile.

At last Trick pulled away and stood up, backing away self-consciously. "Well, there was a Hallmark moment I'm sure you could have lived without."

"It's been an intense few days, Sweets." Bast found his own feet, shivering slightly. "You still want a smoothie? The ice cream's soft enough now."

"I'm staying?" The question was posed in a painfully neutral voice.

"I'd like that, if you're willing." Bast looked at Trick and then at the fruits on a counter. "I enjoy your company, your laugh and God knows we're good in bed. I... I'd like to be friends, Trick. No pressure, no mindfucks. Friends."

"Yeah, okay. That sounds good." Trick's hand found his and squeezed. "But if I'm staying, you're going to have to stock more of the four essential food groups. I mean this chicken and fruit stuff is nice, but where's the fat? The salt? The sugar? And if you're going to keep me coming like this, I'm going to need some nice juicy steaks."

Bast chuckled, squeezing Trick's hand for a second before moving to throw some pineapple and orange juice in the blender with a packet of powdered protein, handing Trick the second carafe to make his smoothie in. "Make a list, Sweets, and remember, don't order what you can't cook."

Trick snorted. "You don't cook junk food -- or steak, for that matter. You just kind of throw it in the pan long enough to make the outside look cooked and then you mop the blood up with bread."

"Do you know that there are places you can buy blood pie? *Very* interesting." Bast poured his juice into a tall glass and pushed the blender over to Trick.

"I don't know." Trick threw fruit, ice and ice cream into the blender. "It kind of sounds weird without the meat to go with it."

"Well, it's not my favorite way to get nutrition, that's for sure." Bast sipped at his juice, throwing the odds and ends that eating caused into the trash, watching what was rapidly becoming his favorite way to get nutrition make breakfast.

The noise of the blender filled the tiny kitchen and then Trick was pouring his smoothie into a glass and downing half of it in a single gulping swallow. He had a pink ice-cream moustache when he turned to Bast.

Bast grinned and waggled his eyebrows. "Got milk?"

"Huh? Oh!" Trick looked sheepish and licked the moustache away. "Meanwhile, you look like you're freezing your ass off, and that would really put a crimp in my plans."

"Yeah? What plans?" Bast finished his juice and moved over to press his chilled body against Trick's. Trick was warm and relaxed and felt delicious against his skin.

"Fuck, you're cold." Trick's arm came around his shoulders, pulling him closer.

"Yeah, I've had a slow metabolism for decades. Takes me a while to warm up." Bast nestled close, nuzzling at Trick's skin. "Wanna huddle under the covers?"

Trick finished his smoothie and rinsed the glass out. "Yeah, huddling under the covers is conducive to my plans, anyway."

Bast grinned and dove for the bed, burying himself beneath the covers.

Trick joined him a moment later, spooning up behind him, arms wrapping around him. The boy was warm and close, hands wandering idly over his skin. "You promised me Bugs Bunny."

"Well, then, you will have it." He reached for the remote and clicked, warm and lazy and settled deep in his bones.

There was something about his Sweets that just felt... right. There wasn't really any other way to explain it. Trick nuzzled against his neck and settled, soft laughter and softer hands, sliding over his skin.

***

Trick let himself out of the warehouse, eyes squinting at the dawn. He hadn't realized until just now that it had been almost a week since he'd even seen the sun.

A week full of laughter and fun and fucking and sleeping and eating whatever he wanted, whenever he was hungry. He hadn't worried about the cops coming or whether or not it was raining or if he was going to have enough money for a Coke and some breakfast. Everything had been taken care of by Bast. He kind of liked it. He kind of liked it a lot.

That scared the shit out of him.

In just a week he'd let go all of his rules; he'd even given up waiting for the other shoe to drop.

He'd finally told Bast that he had to go, there were people expecting to see him, who'd raise a ruckus if they didn't. He had people who cared about him -- he did! Granted, most of then cared more about whether or not they could claim his spot on the mattress and use his blanket than whether or not he disappeared for weeks on end, but they'd still notice if he was gone.

It gave him a chance to get out, get away, prove to himself he wasn't digging himself in too deep with Bast. It was a great ticket and he was just riding it as far as it would take him, right?

He was already beginning to sweat by the time he slipped into the apartment they were squatting in. With no electricity, it was warmer inside than it was out, no wind to cool things off, and it smelled of rancid sweat and cheap booze.

"Trick? Jesus Christ! Is that you, man? Where you been?" Izzy was sprawled out with Mikki and Leeta, ratty blankets bundled all beneath them. His iced-blue hair was skewed and pointing all directions. The kid looked liked he'd spent the night in a clothes-dryer. Who knew, maybe he had.

The sun blazed through the broken windows, promising one of those blistering days that reminded you why you'd want to risk whatever was at home for a few months. Or maybe risk putting all your eggs in one basket.

"Been over in the warehouse district. Found a kid who likes to dance and play, been hanging out with him." He shrugged, watching Izzy's reaction warily.

"Wicked! There room for more than one?"

"Nope." Where the hell had that come from? For all he knew, Bast would be ecstatic to have a couple of guys on tap, but he didn't want to share. It wasn't like he was selfish -- there'd been a time or two when a john had wanted a three-way and he'd been more than happy to call on one of his friends. Hell, there was a safety in numbers. Yet here he was, telling Izzy it wasn't gonna happen like he knew it.

Izzy's face fell and the boy sighed. "Too fucking bad, man. I coulda used a good shag and a good meal ticket. So, is he through with you then, your new kid?"

Trick didn't have to think about it; he knew Bast wasn't through with him, he was welcome to stay -- that much had been clear. What wasn't was for how long that would hold true. "Not yet."

One pierced eyebrow arched. "Then what the fuck are you doing *here*, man?"

It was a damn good question.

"I don't know, man." He shrugged. "Reality check?"

Mikki raised her head; one of her eyes was swollen shut, mottled blue and green. "Reality, asshole? It's fucking hot. We're fucking hungry. And it's fucking early. Good enough for you?"

Izzy chuckled. "Pretty damned real to me, Trick baby."

"Yeah. Yeah, it is."

He dug into his pocket and found a couple of fives. He tossed them to Izzy. "For breakfast for all of you -- to apologize for waking you guys up so early."

And because he was gonna take the plunge and trust that Bast wasn't gonna decide tomorrow that he was through with Trick. And if he did... well, it had been a hell of a week.

Chapter Five

He sent some emails here and there, did a little work, watched Trick sleep, brushed out his hair, watched a Rotato informercial, watched Trick sleep.

Eventually Trick was going to notice. The only reason he hadn't already was that he didn't want to.

The fucking, the laughing, the dancing, the movies and showers and blowjobs and oh, sweet gods, the drunken chocolate of blood -- it was fabulous. But Bast couldn't hide down here forever and, at some point, the slow metabolism and sun allergy stories were going to stop working. Not to mention Bael, who was getting worried, and Rose, who was getting hungry, and Bear, who was getting tired of Bael and Rose's bitching...

He'd pushed it weeks longer than he thought he could.

Bast looked up at his painting -- he'd been carrying it around, putting it up above his bed for what? Three hundred years? Four? Hoping that it would bring him luck, his own personal talisman against pain and heartache and loss.

Bryce had always been a shitty good-luck charm.

"Make or break, Sebastian old boy." He sighed and stood to go make coffee.

Trick was gonna need it.

Whether it was the smell of the coffee, or Trick was just done sleeping, he didn't know, but just as the light came on the machine, indicating it was ready, Trick started to wake up. There was the slow blinking -- two, maybe three times -- and then bam, Trick would be wide awake. At least he didn't bolt upright anymore, hadn't done since about the second week he'd stayed.

"Hey, Sweets. Sleep well?" He hadn't been scared in two hundred years, shouldn't be scared now.

But he was.

Trick sat up and stretched his arms over his head, yawning widely. He grinned over at Bast and then winked. "Slept like I'd been ridden hard and left exhausted."

Bast poured two cups of coffee and wandered over. "Exhausted is a fabulous look on you, Sweets."

Trick took one of the cups and let it sit in his hands, warming them. "Oh, I get it now -- you've been trying to wear me out 'cause I look so good tired. I can think of worse reasons to have sex."

He chuckled. "There are *always* reasons to have sex, Sweets. If you can't find one, you're not thinking hard enough."

Bast settled up next to Trick on the bed, drinking his coffee and trying to remember what he'd said when he'd told Bael, if it had been this hard. He didn't think it had been. For one thing, he hadn't left it so long. For another, Bael believed in the supernatural, in voodoo and strange happenings. Trick didn't seem to believe in anything but himself.

Trick shifted so that they were touching all along their sides, hand sliding over Bast's thigh. He looked at Trick's hand, tan and healthy against his pale skin. Of course, he hadn't fallen in love with Bael either.

He leaned over, pressing close and gathered his courage. "Hey, Sweets, we have something to discuss. My birthday's coming up and I'm a bit older than you'd imagine."

"Your birthday? Oh, cool, are you going to have a party?" Trick gave him a nudge. "I figured out pretty quick you're not 16 -- not living like you do. My mom used to grumble about Lacy Carter, they lived next door and Lacy was way older'n mom, but she had good skin. So what are you? Nineteen? Twenty? Twenty-two?"

"749."

Trick laughed, nearly choking on his coffee. "Good one."

Bast looked over. "It's true. I'm an old guy, born 1352, outside of Athens."

"Oh, come on, Bast. You might look good for your age, but there's no way you look *that* good."

"Well, there are some benefits to my particular medical problem, Trick." He shrugged. "Great skin tone's one of them."

Trick just looked at him for a long time and Bast could see him trying to decide if Bast was fucking with him, crazy, or something in between.

"So let me get this straight -- you think you're 740... what was it? 9? You really believe that?"

Oh, this was going to get worse before it got better.

"Yeah. I've got some semblance of paperwork -- not sure exactly how that'll help though, what I've got's in Greek and they didn't exactly do birth certificates, per se... oh, shit, this is more complicated with someone who isn't in the culture already. I'm sort of out of practice."

Trick frowned. "I don't know anything about Greek culture, but if you want me to, I can learn, right? Or is it because I'm not Greek myself? Is this some weird sort of break-up thing?"

"Fuck, no. No, I don't want to break up and I'm not talking about Greek culture." He took a deep breath. "I'm talking more about my medical condition, really. I'm mean, you have to have noticed that I don't really eat, don't go out in the sun..." Fuck this sounded stupid as shit.

"Just look." He raised his face, letting his eyes change, his teeth, his body, letting his hunger show. And then he hid it away again. "I'm not shitting you, Trick. I'm not your average guy."

"Fuck!" Trick had backed away slightly, looking like he was judging whether or not he could grab his clothes on the way to the elevator. "What the fuck was that?"

"That was the payment for the great skin tone." Bast didn't try to touch him. "One of them, anyway."

"Just tell me what the fuck you are."

"People like me have been called lots of things, Sweets. Vampire is the one bandied about these days." As Trick's eyebrows went up, he nodded. "Yeah, I drink blood. It keeps me alive. But I don't hurt anybody, don't kill anybody."

Trick got up and started to pace around. "You're serious. You're fucking serious. Shit, I've been waiting for the other shoe to drop. This was too fucking sweet, but it was sweet long enough I was starting to believe in it. And then you get all serious and I'm thinking, shit, here it comes. Only, I never in a million years would have guessed what it really was. Shit. I don't even... I can't even... How the hell is this real?"

"Nothing's different, Sweets. It's sort of like a virus, except you have to be given it, you don't just catch it. I got it when I was a kid. I was dying and my governess was... well... one of us... except I wasn't one of us yet." He wanted to go put some clothes on, but he didn't want to move, didn't want to scare Trick. Scare him any worse, anyway.

Trick paced the length of the room twice more and then stopped at the foot of the bed. "This is insane. It's just too... unreal. Show me again."

"Okay." Bast changed again, eyes flaring, need and hunger surged to the forefront. It was easy, to hunger for Trick, to want him. The need singing inside.

"Shit." The word was shaky, Trick sinking down onto the divan. "You're... you're really a vampire. Like, for real."

Trick looked around suddenly. "There's not any cameras or anything -- this isn't some sick joke, right?"

"No joke. No cameras. No shit." Fuck, he wanted Trick. Hungered for him.

"Shit." Trick stared at him for a long moment, looking like he was trying not to cry. "Shit."

Bast let his face relax. "Please Sweets. I'm not any different now than I was last night. I've not hurt you, have I?"

"I didn't know you were a killer last night! What are you doing, fattening me up? Keeping me on tap until you need to suck my blood?"

He blinked, shocked. "I'm not... I've never killed anyone. Ever. I wouldn't. I don't need to."

"You don't need to drink blood to live?"

"I don't need to kill anybody." Bast chuckled, the sound dry. "Fuck, Sweets. Volunteers aren't my problem. It feels *good* when I do it." He swallowed hard, not sure now whether to say anything about the fact that he'd tasted Trick -- had from the very beginning.

Trick was frowning hard now, he could see his Sweets' brain working hard behind the blue eyes. "Shit. You told me once, right at the beginning, that you were a vampire. Fuck. You've been sucking my blood all along, haven't you?"

Trick was up again, pacing, this time with short, sharp steps. His Sweets was angry.

"I didn't lie to you. I have drunk from you, but I never hurt you. *Never.*"

"But you never told me what you were fucking doing -- you never once *asked.*"

His heart sank. It had never been this hard.

"I'm sorry, Sweets. I... I was hungry for you and you were so close and so good." He moved to the edge of the bed, reaching his hand out. "I never hurt you, Trick. I never would."

"How do I know that?" Trick looked around and located his jeans, tossed away in a fit of passion just last night. He pulled them on, staying out of range. "Shit, this is just fucked."

"Please, Trick." Bast stood, a ball of ice in his belly, desperate for his robe. "Please. I'm sorry. I needed to tell you the truth. I *needed* to. Don't go."

Trick shifted, taking a couple of steps back. "You needed to tell me the fucking truth from the beginning! Shit, I should never have come back here with you after that first time. Fuck. Fuck. Fuck."

"The first time? Fuck, Trick, what was I supposed to do?" He held out his hand. "Hi, you're a whore, I'm a vampire. Wanna?" This was unreal, horrid. He didn't want to do this. He wanted to be back in bed with Trick wrapped around him.

"At least that way I would have known what I was getting into! Instead of pretending you were just a normal boy like anyone else and all the time you're sucking my blood!"

Trick slid along the wall over to the dresser and started rummaging until he came up with a black t-shirt, slipping it on as quickly as possibly. "You're not even human! You're like some animal preying on people."

He stopped short, ice spreading, shaking his head. "I'm not an animal. Fuck, I've never touched anyone, *anyone* who didn't want it, didn't want me. Even you, Trick. You never pulled away. Not once."

"You never told me what you were fucking doing! You never gave me the choice to pull away!" Trick was still sliding along the wall, keeping an eye on him as he went for his jacket.

"Please, Trick. Don't go. Stay here and talk about this with me." He walked over, putting himself right in front of Trick. "We've been together for months, Sweets. We've had a good time. Please. Stay and we'll talk."

"Don't touch me!" Trick glared at him, and Bast couldn't help but think of the way animals would puff themselves up all big when they were trying to make themselves look tough and send a don't-mess-with-me message.

"Please. I'm not going to hurt anybody." He spread out his hands. "I've lived here in this city for years -- decades -- and never hurt anyone." He hurt inside, so cold, so far away from center he didn't think he'd find it again.

"Decades... fuck -- you're ancient, fucking hundreds of years old. And I don't know a fucking thing about you -- you've been hiding everything about you that was real." Trick laughed suddenly, and the sound hurt it was so sharp. "You want to know the really funny thing? I was starting to believe that I wasn't just a plaything, that maybe we had something going between us here. What a joke. Haha, Trick -- fooled you."

"I wasn't playing with you, Trick." He reached out, wanting to touch, to comfort. "I haven't hidden from you. *I'm* real. The rest is just details."

Bast needed. Oh, fuck, what he needed was right here. *Right* here.

"Just details? And are you going to eke those details out one at a time, slowly, wait until I'm comfortable and trusting and starting to fa-- and happy and then just lay the next thing on me -- see how long you can con me into staying?" Trick scooted away, skirting his arm. "No, don't touch me. I don't ever want you to touch me again. You're a monster."

"No." Tears welled in his eyes. He wasn't a monster. He wasn't. "Please, Trick."

His heart echoed with the dozens of times he'd said those words.

Parakalo, Elizabeta.

Per favore, Carlo.

S'il vous plait, Michele.

Please, Bryce.

Please.

"Yes, you are. And now that I know I don't want anything more to do with you." Trick glared at him as he walked backward toward the elevator. "I'm gonna go now and you'd better not show your face around Roman street -- we're all gonna have stakes and carry holy water. We don't need any freaks like you down there."

He lifted his chin, looking closely at Trick. He looked carefully, memorizing each feature like he had so many times before, with so many lovers. Trusting people assured that at some point you needed to move on. "You won't see me again. You have my word."

"Like I can believe you." Trick never turned his back on Bast, fumbling for the grating and backing into the elevator once he'd opened it.

"Goodbye, Sweets."

Fear didn't look good on Trick. Of course, neither did hatred, and together they were brutal.

The grating closed on Trick and the elevator began to groan, hiding the sound of Bast's sobs. He reached up, wiping his cheeks, sobs dying when his hands pulled away, covered with blood-stained tears. He wasn't human; he was a monster.

And if he didn't want the villagers coming with their pitchforks and flaming torches, it was time to get the hell out of Dodge.

It took three phone calls -- one to his sister, one to his lawyer and one to Bael -- to transfer papers, money, everything away from here, leave it for the person most likely to come back to hunt them. It took twenty minutes to pack the most conservative clothes he owned, his software, papers and laptop, and pull Bryce's painting off the wall.

It took another hour for Bael to come down the elevator to take him to his new home.

Bael turned almost white when he walked out of the bathroom wearing Jacob Sebastian's new face -- black slacks, white turtleneck, black jacket, no makeup. His hair was black again -- at least what was left of it. The last foot of it or so was in the trash.

"Hey, pretty." He forced himself to smile. "Thanks for the ride."

"No problem, Bast."

"Jacob now, pretty."

"J...Jacob. You..." Bael swallowed. "You gonna be okay?"

"Of course, pretty one. Just trusted the wrong one, you know. Bound to happen. I'm ready to go now. I won't be back, if the moon is willing." He handed Bael the painting and grabbed his bags. He looked back at their bed, their home. No, Trick's now. He didn't belong here anymore.

Bast was a dead man.

He put an envelope on the bar and smiled over at his friend. "C'mon. I'll show you around uptown. I need to do some shopping."

He followed Bael into the elevator and didn't look back. There was nothing to see.

Chapter Six

He'd been halfway to Bast's a dozen times in the last three days. A dozen times he'd turned and gone back home.

Back home to the mattress on the floor shared by a dozen people. Back home to the cold and the dirt and the never being warm enough or full enough.

Or held.

Or cared for.

Fucked into oblivion.

Fuck, he missed Bast.

Not because the guy was rich or good looking or fucked like a dream, but because he was Bast and Trick had gotten used to his company, gotten comfortable with it, come to expect it, come to need it. He liked being around the other boy... vampire.

Oh, he'd been shocked. Surprised. He hadn't believed it.

It didn't make sense, but it was real enough. He'd seen it with his own eyes. Bast was a monster.

A seven hundred and fifty year-old monster.

A beautiful monster.

A monster he was falling in falling for

A monster.

If he said it often enough, maybe he'd believe it, maybe he'd forget the look in Bast's eyes as he told him he never wanted to see Bast ever again. If he said it enough maybe he would stop hurting, stop needing, stop wanting.

It was three days before he admitted to himself that he was more hurt that Bast had kept secrets from him than he was angry over what that secret was. Then it had taken another day before he'd decided that pride didn't keep you warm at night and pride didn't hold you and pride sure as hell didn't make you scream with pleasure.

He went all the way to Bast's this time, playing with the elevator key-card in his front pocket, fingers stroking it, touching it, his link to Bast.

He spent at least a half hour standing in front of the elevator, working up the nerve to go down and face Bast. If he was the vampire, he wouldn't want to see himself, that was for sure.

Finally he was in the elevator, moving down, the contraption groaning and moaning like it was dying.

"I'm sorry, please hear what I have to say before you kick me out." He said it loudly as he opened the grate.

His voice echoed and the air smelled weird -- stale and still. Even before he looked above the big bed and saw the huge lighter green square on the wall where the painting had been, he knew Bast was gone. The apartment had that odd, disinfected look to it, like an apartment showroom or a hotel room. One that wasn't Bast.

Not his Bast at all.

Fuck.

There had to be something... some clue.

He could go looking, try at Bast's usual hang outs, but shit, he'd look like an idiot, asking around if anyone has seen Bast, and it was a shot in the dark. He prowled around the place twice before he noticed the white envelope on the bar.

There was a 'T.' scrolled across the front, rich and black against the paper. He was almost scared to open it. He was more scared not to.

The envelope was full of what looked like legal papers, typed and signed and stuff. Trick looked through them with a frown, looking for something from Bast. He didn't want legal mumbo-jumbo, he wanted to know where Bast was, dammit.

The letter, when he found it, looked painfully short.

"Sweets,

"These are the temporary deeds to the apartment, the warehouse upstairs. The final deeds should be mailed to you soon via my attorney. The bills are paid by the income from the guys upstairs. Mr. Leonid runs things. He's brilliant. I'd keep him on. It's your place now.

"I'm sorry. I never meant to hurt you.

"B."

Fuck.

He didn't want the apartment, he wanted Bast.

He sank down to the floor, clutching the papers. Looking around the place, he shook his head. This wasn't his. It would never be his, especially not without Bast.

It was a while later before it occurred to him that leaving the apartment to him, writing him the letter, these meant that maybe Bast still cared about him. All he needed to do was find him.

He frowned, wondering where to start.

His eyes happened across the phone and he went over and picked it up. There was still a dial tone. He hit redial.

The phone rang four or five times before a soft, southern drawl answered. "Bast, babe? I thought you weren't calling me from that number, honey? Thought you were in hibernation mode. You hungry, babe? Lonely?"

Oh, fuck. Bast had another lover.

Of course he did, he was 750 fucking years old -- he probably had thousands of lovers, old, new, alive and dead and... shit, Trick hadn't thought *that* would hurt so much.

The voice stopped and then resumed, more cautious. "Bast? Now come on, I know you're hurting over the pretty boy, honey, but you gotta stop crying and heartbreaking over him. Come on, Bast. Talk to me, talk to your old friend Bael."

Bast was crying and heartbreaking over him?

There was hope.

Now how to get the guy on the other end of the phone to give up the address of Bast's new living space.

He made a non-commital, choked, sobbing kind of sound, hoping a little of his own pain would be mistaken for Bast's.

"Oh, Bast... What did that evil asshole do to our happy dancing boy, huh? I've never seen those eyes sad. Tell me -- what do you need? Food? Company? Dancing? More shopping for that high-brow apartment? Fucking? What?"

The fucking address of that high-brow apartment. How the fuck did he get this guy to give up Bast?

"I..." Then it hit him, have this guy come to *him*. "Forgot something," he rasped in little more than a whisper, hoping this guy would put it down to tears.

"In the warehouse flat? You shoulda called. I'd have fetched it." The voice was getting concerned, worried.

"Some papers... got them now." Trick crossed his fingers, hoping the guys would buy it.

"Are you there? At the old place? You need a ride or something?" He heard the voice talking quick and worried to someone and then it returned. "Look, you're not making sense. You haven't eaten in what? A week at least? I'm coming down to pick you up and take you back home. You can't stay there, babe. What if he comes with a bunch of guys, leaves you broken out in the sun, yeah? I'm coming for you. You sit tight and let Bael take care of you, babe."

"K." He hung up the phone, hand shaking.

Now he had to figure out what he was going to do when this guy showed up.

Looking around, he folded the papers carefully and stuffed them back into the envelope and set it on the bar. That was all he'd touched besides the phone. He went over to the elevator and pressed himself against the wall, waiting anxiously.

It didn't take nearly as long as he thought it would before the familiar, slow grind of the elevator started down.

When the grate opened and this *Bael* stepped out, Trick was almost surprised to recognize the tall, thin black man. The few times Trick had seen Bast outside the apartment this guy had always been with somebody else, but nearby. Like Bast's shadow.

"Bast? You in here, babe? Everything okay?"

He still didn't have a plan, so he just winged it. Pouncing, he slammed the man back against the grating, arm going across the big man's windpipe. "Where is he?"

"Who the *fuck* are you?" The tall guy struggled, thin hands pushing at his arm.

"Just tell me where Bast is." He pushed harder with his hand over Bael's windpipe.

"Kiss my ass. He doesn't want to see you." The dark eyes were angry now instead of scared, stubborn and pissed off.

Well, shit, he'd played that wrong. He didn't let the black guy go though. He glared stubbornly back. "Yes he does. And we both know it."

"No. He doesn't. And even if he did I wouldn't tell you." Bael snorted. "I've known Bast for fifteen years. Never seen him cry. Never seen him *unhappy* once. Until you."

"He's unhappy because I'm not with him -- he wants his Trick." Trick let go and stepped back, letting his weight settle on one leg, knowing it showed him to advantage. "You're going to deny him a chance to get all this back?"

Bael arched an eyebrow. "Look, I know you're for rent and I know Bast's a solid ticket. Hell, you blew that on your own. I know, but Bast didn't get it." Bael shrugged and started pacing, looking all upperclass in his jeans and blue silk shirt.

"He didn't get that you don't owe somebody worry and care and concern when you're paying them to fuck you." Bael looked at Trick. "At some fucked up point, Bast forgot what you are and that was a mistake. But you've been paid -- an apartment, a fucking warehouse, more than you'd ever make. He's paid his fucking debt to you, willed you Sebastian Apostolos' life. Bast is dead, Trick. Leave him in his grave."

Trick snarled. "Then get the fuck out off *my* property -- you're breaking and entering." He wanted to scream -- he'd not taken a dime from Bast, not since that first time, but he would never admit to this asshole that he'd gotten soft himself.

"Happy to." Bael opened the grate and walked in, slamming it down behind him. As the elevator began to move, he turned. "Leave Bast alone. He's not a monster. And he's not yours."

After the elevator took the black man away, Trick sat down hard, staring unhappily at the empty space behind the grating.

He stayed there until his tears stopped and then he went and splashed his face. Before he left, he put his elevator card next to the envelope and walked away.

***

He'd stopped moping after about three days, then he started working, frantically, mindlessly. All the little things he'd let slide while he and Tri... while he was busy got finished and settled and fixed and paid for.

Then Bast went through the tedious business of killing one personage and building himself another. It had been a stupid risk, trusting Trick, but he figured he needed an excuse to change, an excuse to reinvent. Maybe he'd head to the west coast, play with the children there.

He looked down at his rumbling belly, belt already loose around it. Or maybe he'd just lock himself into the main room with its floor-to-ceiling windows and wait to die.

The bell rang, startling him enough that he almost dropped his coffee.

Pushing the button, he finished the last few gulp. "Yes?"

"Home delivery -- someone here order a fresh pint?" Bael's soft tones were made flat by the intercom.

"Hey, pretty one. Come on up."

He let Bael in, not sure if he was happy for the company or not. His fingers pulled through his short hair, missing the feel of the long strands. Trick liked it purple, liked to touch it, liked...

He shook his head as he made for the door, opening it to a smiling face.

"Hey, babe, you're looking good." Bael lied to him and stepped in and bent to kiss him, tongue warm as it pushed into his lips.

He reached up to wrap his arms around Bael's neck, groaning. Two weeks since he'd touched somebody. Two weeks since he'd fed. Two weeks and he was desperate and hungry.

Bael's hands were soft, stroking and warm. "Take what you need, babe -- I'm here for you."

"Bael... pretty... so good to me." He was weeping again, with hunger and need and the knowledge that this wasn't what he wanted, not really.

"That's what people who care for each other do, Bast. You know I love you." Bael was backing them slowly toward a low divan. "Now, come on, feed."

He almost crawled up Bael's body, straddling the thin hips when they sat down. Bael's head was already lifted, vein pulsing as his hunger fought free and he struck, biting deep.

Bael groaned, the sound deep and solid, the big body jerking with pleasure.

He drank deep, pulling the sweet, hot blood into him until that aching in his belly faded, then he eased the wound shut.

Then he collapsed into Bael's arms, with an exhausted sob. "Thank you."

"How long since you last had anything?" Bael's big hands were stroking him, moving over his touch-starved body. "You should have called sooner -- I would have come."

"So good to me. Just been busy. Just been... oh, your hands, pretty. It's good." He stayed close, drinking in one sensation after another, almost shuddering in reaction.

"Oh, babe, it hurts me to see you like this, to see you suffering for that little whore."

"Sh... don't, Bael. My fault. I was stupid. It's over. All over." He wasn't at a place where he could call Trick a whore, not yet.

He raised his head for a kiss, just needing the contact. Bael's lips closed over his, warm and easy. Not Trick, but good and familiar and caring and they'd do.

"You gonna let me love you, pretty?" Bael asked, large hands roaming over him.

"Let you do anything, Bael, just keep touching me. I'm so lonely here." He knew he was whining and didn't even care, just wanted contact, touch.

Bael made a deep-throated growling noise and stood, picking him up easily. "Bedroom?"

He pointed listlessly, almost asleep. He hoped Bael wasn't looking for acrobatics. He wasn't even sure he could get it up.

He almost missed it when Bael got them onto the bed and he looked up into the familiar painting, the only real thing he had left. "Bast...?"

There was a sigh and one of the big, warm hands slid over his head and cupped his cheek softly. Then he was enveloped in warmth, Bael curling around him. "Sleep. I'll watch over you."

Bast nodded, already dreaming of Trick's eyes.

Chapter Seven

It took Trick almost a month to find Bael again.

He spent as much time as he could, hanging out around the places he knew Bast used to frequent, hoping the big black man would show up. Finally he did.

He'd learned from his past mistakes, though, hadn't let the guy even see him this time, let alone confront him. For seven hours he trailed Bael from one nightclub to the next, including a bad few hours when he thought he'd been spotted and ducked out on.

At last he trailed the big man home.

When all the lights went out, he debated going and finding some work and some food, but he couldn't risk Bael going to see Bast while he was gone. For all he knew Bael wouldn't even lead him to Bast. Maybe Bast had left the city. Maybe even the country.

He hoped not.

He'd follow Bael around for another four weeks if he had to, waiting for the man to lead him to Bast.

He hunkered down in a quiet alley across from Bael's place, pretty confident the hunger pangs would keep him awake.

Thank goodness the man lived close to the action. He'd have been lost if he'd had to take a bus or a cab ; he was dead broke.

Fuck, he was a fool.

Almost four months with Bast and not a damn thing to show for it. He hadn't told anyone about the warehouse that he'd left behind, they'd call him all sorts of a fool, but he just couldn't take it; it wasn't why he'd stayed with Bast. Hell, he was calling himself all sorts of a fool. He wasn't even sure why he wouldn't take anything from Bast -- he had to eat, he didn't like being a $10 whore, but he just... couldn't.

If Bast refused to see him...

He shivered and curled in on himself. Fuck, it was cold.

The sun had been up for hours before Bael ventured out again, and Trick wound up following him all over the fucking neighborhood. Dry cleaning picked up, groceries bought, lunch eaten. Trick had watched every single bite going into Bael's mouth. Then home again.

He was ready to scream. He wasn't sure he could do another long, cold night and another day of aimless wandering. But he was equally sure that he couldn't *not* do it.

The sun had just started going down when Bael came out of the building again, turning, not toward downtown and the clubs, but uptown, walking briskly, with a purpose.

Trick followed hopefully, the hope growing when Bael disappeared inside a tall high-rise. Going to the front, he searched the names. There it was. It had to be. Jacob Sebastian.

He ducked back along the street, collecting flowers from the lobby of the next building over and waiting for Bael to come back out. Surprisingly, he didn't have long to wait and, once Bael had turned the corner, Trick went and rang the buzzer for Jacob Sebastian.

"Yes?" Oh, fuck. It was him. Right here, rich voice turned flat by the intercom.

"Got a delivery for a Bast here." He laid on an accent, not too thick, he hoped. "Flowers. Is this the right place?"

"Bast?" Flat and suspicious -- Bast didn't sound particularly willing to buzz anyone up. "Who from?"

"Card says love Rose and this is the address I was given." He could remember Bast mentioning a Rose once or twice, said they should get together with her and the gang soon. It was a shot in the dark; if it didn't work he'd try something else. "Look, if you don't want 'em I've got other deliveries to make before I can get home, man."

There was no answer, just the buzz of the door opening. The lobby was all silver and green, stark and bare and cold. Completely different from the warehouse. Trick knew the elevators to the fourteenth floor would be quick and silent.

It took no time at all for the elevator to get there and he stepped out, checking the corridors and going right. Second door. He was here.

Still clutching the flowers tightly in front of him, and why he thought he actually needed the flowers for this ruse he wasn't sure, he knocked on the door. Fuck, he felt like he was going to throw up.

When Bast opened the door, he forgot about the flowers, about throwing up.

Bast looked like he was dying.

The sparkle, the color, the sexy, slinky charisma -- it was either hidden or dead behind this short-haired, empty-eyed, hollow-cheeked, turtle-necked boy.

Without so much as a word, Bast closed the door.

Oh, fuck, he'd done that. He was killing Bast as surely as if he'd pulled him into the sunshine. Well, it was time to drag Bast back into the shadows, if the vampire would let him.

Leaning his whole body against the door, Trick pressed his palms and cheek flat against it. He was pretty sure Bast could hear him, no matter how quiet he was, and he didn't want anyone calling the cops on him so he whispered.

"Please, baby-boy, you have to let me in. Please. Bast. I know you can hear me. I'm not going until you let me in."

"Oh, Sweets... I can't. You have to go." Soft and broken and filled with an ache Trick was only beginning to understand, Bast's voice was close, he could almost feel the heat of Bast's body pressed against his, with only the lacquered door in their way.

"Bast..." His voice was thick with the tears that were running down his cheeks and it felt like something inside was dying. "Don't make me go back out there without you. Please, I need you. I need the flavor of your mouth and the touch of your fingers."

The door opened a crack, quiet dark eyes looking out at him. "I can't be what I'm not. I can't watch the dawn. I can't be just a man. I never lied to you, not really." A single tear slid down the hollowed cheeks. "I didn't mean to care for you, Trick. I just wanted to play. I didn't know I would need you."

"I tried to go back out there by myself, Bast. I really truly did. I don't want to need you, to want you, but I do. There isn't a part of me that doesn't yearn for your touch." He held out his arm and pulled back his sleeve, exposing his wrist, his veins blue against pale skin. "Please."

"Oh, God, Trick..." Dark eyes flashed bright for a moment, a fierce hunger tinged with desperate need crossing Bast's face. He shook his head, backing away from the door, retreating into the sterile room. "I can't. Don't offer."

He pushed the door open and followed -- Bast had left it open, and Trick took that as invitation. "Why not? You may have never lied about it, but you never told me about it in a way you expected me to believe and so I didn't know, not really. But you fed from me. You didn't ask, you didn't give me a chance to say no. And now that I'm here, now that I'm offering it freely and knowing what I'm offering, you don't want it?" His voice had gone shrill and he was shaking, and he fell silent with a curse; he'd told himself he wouldn't do this, that he wouldn't accuse or beg or fight, he'd just come and state his case and be cool. *Oh, yeah, Trick, you're being real cool.*

"I want you, more than I've wanted anyone in three hundred years, maybe even longer." Bast wandered over to the windows, looked down at the lights of the city. He looked strange, distant and lost. "I'm sorry. I should have walked away that first night. Should have just turned and run. Should never have tasted your lips."

"Yeah, well, you don't get do-overs, baby-boy. Not even you. You want me, I want you. What's the problem? Yes, I was nasty and mean when I found out, but what did you expect -- me to go 'oh, cool, let's get busy?' Six weeks ago, I didn't even know vampires were *real*. But now I know you are and I'm still here, willing." He could feel the stupid tears trying to come back as he stared at Bast's stiff back, and he wiped angrily at his eyes. "Give me one good reason why you're running away."

Bast looked up at him and suddenly the boy was gone, replaced by old, tired eyes that couldn't remember what truth or satisfaction felt like. "Because I am falling for you, Trick. Because I could get used to needing you. Somehow I don't think you're a long-term relationship kind of guy."

Trick's jaw tightened and somehow he managed not to let the tears fall, though they burned like flames in his eyes. "Yeah, that's right. I'm more the one-night-stand fuck-for-a-buck kind of guy." He nodded and shrugged, pulling on his street face like a cloak. "You'd think I'd be better at knowing when to take my money and run. I won't bother you again, Mr. Sebastian." He turned on his heel and headed for the door. It was so far away. He hadn't come in that far -- just across the threshold, he'd thought.

"It was never about money, Sweets." Bast's voice was broken and quiet, deadly serious. "Not with me. I need you. I want you. Fuck, I care so much for you. *That's* what it was about. I never wanted to own your time. Never."

He couldn't turn back around, but he didn't walk out either. "I didn't come back here for the money, Bast."

"Why did you come back?"

"Because the thought of spending the rest of my fucking life without you made me want to step in front of a car."

"You'd be better off just throwing me in front of one." A long, slender hand slid into his. "I'm too fond of your smile to see it mangled."

He couldn't turn, couldn't lean back, couldn't even breathe, but his hand closed around Bast's, the cool skin warming at his touch. "I'm scared." It was little more than a whisper and he could remember saying it once before, telling Bast his innermost secrets all in those two little words.

Oh, but it hurt to flay himself open like that, hurt more than any punch, hurt more than a broken bone or harsh words, hurt more than knowing he was nothing. It wasn't much. Two words. They were probably the bravest thing he'd ever done and he knew he would never lay himself open to anyone like this ever again.

"So am I." Bast's hand squeezed his. "I didn't want to hurt you. I just..."

He felt Bast move, was suddenly presented with ageless, black eyes. "You scare me. What you make me feel scares me."

A shudder went through him, and he couldn't tell if he was relieved or more terrified than ever. "I won't tell anyone if you don't."

"My lips are sealed." A trembling hand stroked over his cheek. "I've missed you, Sweets."

He nuzzled into the soft hand. "I know. I thought I'd be fine, thought you were just a delicious distraction from my life. But it got worse, every day it got worse instead of better."

"Yeah. I ache inside." Bast caressed him, fingers sliding over his skin. "Can I... will you... kiss me, Sweets? Please? Just once?"

Trick shook his head. "No. Not if it's only going to be once."

"Oh..." Bast smiled softly, a stunned look in his eyes as if he couldn't help his pleasure. "I can live with that. How do you feel about every day until you're tired of me?"

"I thought you weren't really alive..." Trick's eyes were closing, his head tilting to the side and down.

"I'm alive... I'm just not dying." He could hear the husky tone to Bast's voice, could almost feel the sharp edge of need.

Trick's eyes closed fully as his mouth met Bast's and suddenly it didn't matter, none of it mattered except for the pure pleasure that poured through him, clinging to every nerve. Bast was liquid in his arms, heat and hunger and the hint of tears. Hands slid into his hair, holding him close as they tasted each others' desire.

"Stay, Trick. Please. I want you to stay."

"Yes." It was funny how one little word could taste like forever.

Bast nuzzled against him, nibbling softly on his lips. "Oh, God, I thought I'd never taste your mouth again."

He raised his hands, sliding them through the shorn hair. "You cut your hair."

"Yeah." Bast shrugged. "I needed to be someone less noticeable, I guess. Someone no one would see."

Trick drew back and tried to look at the vampire with objective eyes. He shook his head. "I don't think that's possible."

"No?" Bast reached up and stroked the underside of Trick's jaw. "You think you would still find me at the club?"

"I could find you with a blindfold on, in a dark room full of people."

"How?" Soft kisses began to fall on his cheek, his chin, his lips. "How would you find me, Sweets?"

"I don't know." He shrugged again, pressing into the kisses. "It's like...I can feel you. The room can look empty but my heart starts pounding and I feel hot and I know you're there."

"Oh, Trick." Bast kissed him, tongue pressing deep into his mouth, tasting him, devouring him. Trick could feel Bast, hard and shuddering, pressed tight against him.

He pulled on Bast's tongue, sucking vigorously, Bast's hips picking up the rhythm. Finally he broke the kiss with a gasp, hands fluttering over Bast's shoulders and back. "You want me, don't you? You want to... feed from me, take me inside you. Fucking shit, that's like... you need me to live."

"Yes. God, yes." The dark eyes flashed again, bright and sharp. "It's like an ache that won't stop without you. Nothing makes it ease but you. But I won't... not if you don't want me to. I can control it, really."

Letting his head drop back, he wrapped his hands in Bast's short hair and pulled his lover's face into his neck. "I want to be inside you like that."

"Oh, fuck. Oh..." A low hungry growl and Bast's body became suddenly slinky. Something sharp and stiff touched his throat and then a warm tongue swiped over his skin. "You're sure? You want this, love?"

"Yes." He hissed, body beginning to vibrate. "Next time I want to be fucking you when you do it."

"Fuck, yes. Yes." Bast sobbed against him, a sharp flash of sensation sparked at his throat and then sheer pleasure poured over him, stronger than anything he'd ever felt, anything he imagined.

He came with a sob, shuddering at the sensations that spoke so purely of Bast. It seemed to go on forever and then he was clinging limply to Bast, light-headedly floating as the vampire licked delicately at his skin.

"Oh, by all the gods, nothing tastes like you. Nothing ever has." Bast led them to the low divan, easing Trick down carefully, hands smoothing over his clothes, his skin. "So good, Sweets. So fucking good."

"Fuck me... that was... " Trick blinked slowly, unable to find the right words. "You've done that before -- a bit. But this was...more, better..." His body arched as a shiver went through him, Bast's hands on his skin drawing the sense memory from his nerves.

"I... it gets stronger when I feel good, when I'm really hungry." Bast settled against him, body warm -- it occurred to Trick suddenly that Bast was warm with *his* blood, with *him*.

He shuddered. "Oh God -- and I thought you were addictive before."

"There are some benefits to being with someone like me."

He curled into the warm body, letting Bast hold him and pet him, bring him slowly down from the height he was floating at.

"Missed your smell, your touch. Missed your skin and how warm you are. Missed waking up next to you." Bast was murmuring softly against his throat, snuggling close.

A part of him knew he didn't deserve this -- he'd been horrible, lashing out and hurting just in case he was on his way to getting hurt himself, but he didn't care. He was going to take this second chance and hold on with everything he had.

No matter what Bast threw at him next.

He slid his hand over Bast's thigh, wishing he was feeling the silk of Bast's skin.

Bast hummed. "Oh! Missed that, too, Sweets. You've lost weight, you hungry? I bet I can get a pizza delivered." Dark, nervous, hopeful eyes met his. "Or a steak."

"I'm starving," he admitted. "I was looking for Bael for a while and once I found him, I didn't want to break for food." What he didn't admit was that it had been weeks since he'd had a decent meal, living mostly on chips and Coke since he'd walked out on Bast.

"Oh." Bast leaned up and gave him a soft kiss. "Thank you."

Then Bast's warmth was gone, moving across the room to the phone. He watched Bast move; he wasn't the only one who'd lost weight. The apartment was stark, as fake and cold and not-Bast as the lobby downstairs. He wondered if the bedroom looked more like the warehouse apartment, more like home. When he had more energy he'd go look, go see if he could find something of his baby-boy in this mausoleum.

"Pizza's coming, Sweets. Loaded all the way." Bast was wandering, looking out the huge windows, looking a little lost. "I'm not a monster, you know. I'm different, odd, weird, but not a monster. I don't hurt people. Ever."

"Fuck. I'm sorry." He stood up in one motion, sitting back down in a hurry as the world started to go black. "Shit. Can you come here, please?"

Bast frowned, hurrying forward. Cool hands settled him back onto his back, stretching him out. "You okay, Sweets? You don't look good. Let me see if Bael left anything here that's edible."

"I'm fine -- I just stood up too quickly. Bast." He held out his hand. "Please. Just come sit with me."

Bast settled, fingers sliding into his. "Okay. Okay, Sweets." Bast's free hand moved over his body, petting and caressing.

"I'm sorry about the things I said. I don't really think you're a monster."

"No? Really? Because I'm not. Really." Bast's eyes were devastated. "Really."

He sat up carefully, relieved when the world didn't spin, and slid his hand along Bast's cheek and up into the shorn hair. "I was angry and scared and determined to be the one leaving, not the one left." Leaning forward he brought their mouths together. "If I really thought you were a monster, I would never have come looking for you."

"Oh, Trick." Bast moved closer, snuggling into Trick's arms. "It's been so long, but you found me."

He held Bast tight, wishing they were naked, wishing they were making love, wishing he'd never said any of those hurtful things.

"I wish we were home." Bast looked up at him, biting the full bottom lip. "Well, the warehouse, I mean."

"Me, too," he whispered, leaning forward and sliding his tongue along that bottom lip. Bast groaned, the heat of his breath brushing over Trick's mouth. Suddenly he was tearing at Bast's clothes, trying to find *his* Bast underneath the sedate turtleneck and the tan pants.

"Sweets..." Bast was gasping, half-helping, half-arching into the touches.

He tried to rip the turtle neck into two, failing miserably, laughing into Bast's mouth as he went for another tactic, pushing the offending material up. Bast's lips left his, the turtleneck pulled up and off, revealing the pale torso to him.

"Better?"

"There's barely anything left of you..." He reached out sliding his hand along the concave belly. "I'm sorry," he whispered.

"Just been dieting a bit." Bast ducked his head, pushing closer. "Girlish figure and all that."

"You should have ordered the steak. I think I'm gonna need it." He dipped his head and licked at one of Bast's nipples. Bast made a fabulous squeak, arching into his mouth, so needy, so hungry. He closed his mouth over the small piece of flesh, tugging it between his lips, tasting Bast, tasting need.

"Oh, fuck." Bast's voice was raw, stunned. "Fuck, Sweets. So good."

"Bast." His hands slid to Bast's pants, undoing them, pushing them off. "Need to fuck you."

"Oh. Oh, yes." Bast kicked his trousers away with a soft sob, thin legs straddling him as Bast moved.

He dug into his pockets. "Shit, I haven't got any condoms left."

"Who the fuck cares, Sweets?" At his raised eyebrow, Bast grinned, the look desperate and wild. "Last I checked, I'm not likely to get fucking pregnant and we're a bit beyond worrying about safe sex, yeah? Hell, I just *drank* your blood, Trick."

He blinked up at Bast for a moment as the words sank in and then grinned. "Oh fuck." He hadn't ridden bareback. Ever.

He slid his hands between them, pulling open his jeans, pushing them off only as far as he had to to free his cock.

Bast's hands were hot on his cock, pulling hard and steady. "Need you."

"Fuck!" He arched up into the cool hands, the slender fingers familiar and missed. "Please, Bast."

"Yes." Bast scooted closer, ass rocking against him, teasing and hot and hungry. The motion made him twist and groan, aching. Then, with a shudder and a groan, Bast sank down onto his cock.

He bucked up, shoving deep into Bast, body shaking with need and hunger. Fuck, it was so good. It was fucking fantastic and he could feel Bast, all silk and heat around him and he couldn't believe how much better it felt without the condom.

Bast's head fell back and he sobbed, thin body riding him with a frenetic pace, long throat working.

He found Bast's cock with his hand, wrapping tight around it, pumping hard. It felt so good, nothing ever felt like this, ever felt so fucking good -- only Bast.

"Trick... Sweets... Oh, fuck." Bast began to rock, grinding down with increasingly loud groans.

He met each movement, pushing up into Bast's body. This was what it was all about, this visceral need that had hold of him and wouldn't let go. He let it carry him away.

Bast jerked, body tightening as seed shot from him, splashing on Trick's hand and belly.

It was the smell that got to him, pushed him barreling over into his orgasm as his nose was full of the musky scent of Bast's pleasure.

Bast fell forward, gasping and cuddling close. "Oh, Sweets. Trick. Missed you."

He wrapped his arms around Bast, holding him close. "Yeah. I know." He pressed a kiss against Bast's forehead. "I know."

"Can we go home after the pizza? I hate this place." Bast was relaxed, soft and warm and nibbling gently against his neck.

"If I can walk by then," he teased. Then it occurred to him. "Have you still got your key card for the elevator? I kind of..." he ducked his head. "I left mine next to your letter. I didn't want the place -- I was never with you for the money, Bast. Never. All right -- that first night, yeah, but after that it was always about you, I never expected anything."

"I just wanted you to have something. To have a home, you know? Your own place." Bast looked up and grinned. "And, yeah, I have a key card. I... I couldn't part with it."

He slid his hand along Bast's face. "After all I said to you, you still wanted that for me?"

"Yeah. I... I wanted you to have a home. Wanted you to have a place."

He brought Bast's face back to his for a kiss. Shit, he was such an asshole.

Bast hummed into the kiss and then pulled away. "You make me hungry."

"Why do I think you don't mean for pizza?"

"No, but I do need to get my provider to start delivering blood to the apartment again." Bast watched him carefully. "I usually drink bagged stuff. It's clean and easy."

"What about the..." he wasn't sure what to call it. "Feeding? From me?"

"What do you mean, Sweets?" Bast reached out, stroked his throat with a trembling hand.

Trick nuzzled into the touch. "It felt good." He grinned suddenly. "But now I know what your amazing sex secret is."

"Maybe one of them. Feeding from you is... you taste like..." Bast shuddered, moved away, holding his stomach. "You're addictive and rich, Sweets. Delicious."

"What's wrong?"

"Nothing. I just want you. I... I haven't eaten regularly and you're like a banquet right in front of..." Bast was interrupted by the intercom. "Dinner's here!"

"I'm more dressed than you are," he said, getting up slowly.

He zipped himself back up. It was only after Bast had buzzed the guy up that he remembered he didn't have any money.

Bast searched through his pants and found a twenty, handing it over the back of the couch. "If I'm going to move into your house, the least I can do is buy food."

He felt his cheeks go red. Pretty slick, claiming he wasn't here for the money and then not even having enough to cover a fucking pizza.

He paid the delivery boy and had the box open and a slice in his hand before the door was even closed behind him. The smell was enough to kill him, all grease and cheese and pepperoni, fuck, he hadn't had anything like this in weeks. He had the first piece finished by the time he was back at the couch.

"You want one?" he asked as he wolfed down a second piece.

"Not my sort of thing, Sweets. Want a Coke or a beer?" Bast had wandered to the bathroom and cleaned up and was now wandering toward the kitchen.

"Coke," he called around another piece. Shit, he was being unbelievably rude, but he was so fucking hungry.

Bast came back, can of Coke in hand, looking at him in a dazed, warm, disbelieving way.

"Thanks." He took the Coke and had a long swig, washing down the fourth piece of pizza he'd wolfed down. There were four more slices left and he was still pretty fucking hungry, but at the same time, his stomach wasn't feeling too pleased about the sudden dump.

"I know you drink fruit juice and protein shakes and stuff -- I never saw you drinking blood back at the warehouse, though. Or eating anything solid -- can you?" Now that he'd accepted it, accepted Bast was a vampire, he was curious. Bast didn't seem anything like the vampires of monster movies.

"I can, but it won't stay down well. I had some bagged stuff, just kept it low and easy. I did... I fed from you a couple of times." Bast met his eyes. "I'm sorry. I should have asked. I was just carried away."

He nodded, and then smiled. "'s'okay -- I forgive you."

He chewed on his lower lip, trying to figure out how to ask the next one. "Are you going to... keep on feeding from me?"

"I won't if you don't want me to. I can do okay on the bags, and Bael and Rose and Bear are always willing, when I need something hot and alive."

He thought about it. It was weird, to think about Bast sucking his blood, that he'd let him, but it felt good, pretty fucking amazing in fact, and then there was the little hollow feeling in his stomach from when Bast talked about getting it from other people, people Trick had never even met. Well, except for Bael, but that hardly counted.

"I liked it, Bast, and I want you to do it again, I just... I need you to ask first."

Bast nodded. "I will, I swear it. I'll never take anything you haven't offered, Trick."

He slid his hand over to Bast's, linking their fingers. "Thanks."

Bast squeezed his fingers and grinned. "You're welcome. Finish your pizza and I'll pack. I want to go home."

He shook his head and shifted the box off his lap. "I'm done."

He looked over at the most definitely not Bast clothes on the end of the divan. "Do you really need to pack? Seems like most of the stuff here doesn't belong to you. Not the real you."

Bast gave him a look, soft and shocked and so hot. Then Trick got a kiss, all tongue and hunger. "Just need my laptop and my painting, Sweets."

"Okay," he said, licking his lips, suddenly wanting again. "Lets get out of here."

"Yeah. Let's go home, Sweets." Bast grinned, eyes alight and happy. "Call us a cab. I'll gather my stuff."

Trick felt his own happiness growing in response to the obvious delight in Bast's. "We're a cab," he said softly, watching Bast's face.

Bast's laugh was free and wild and just like he remembered, dark eyes dancing as he was soundly kissed. "Oh, I did miss you, Sweets."

His arms shot out and circled Bast, holding him close as he took another hard, desperate kiss. "I missed you, too."

He took a deep breath and smiled. "Let's go home, Bast. Take me home."

***

The first things he did when he got home was hang the painting up and call the all-night grocery store for supplies. He'd contact his blood supplier before bed, along with Bael and a real estate agent.

Oh, he'd missed this place. He'd been here almost 40 years, all told, and the land had belonged to him for far longer. Bast blushed. He hadn't mentioned that part to Trick. Of course, there were lots of things about him Trick didn't know yet.

They had time.

Bast bounced onto the bed, all grins. "It's good to be home, yeah?"

Trick offered him a shy smile. "Yeah. And it is home, isn't it -- for both of us?"

He curled onto his side on the mattress, smiling over at his own personal embodiment of sex. "Yeah, Sweets. Yours and mine."

Trick's smile became more easy and he moved over to sit on the bed, hand coming out to stroke along Bast's face. "I feel... I don't know -- like I was a jerk and you let me get away with it." Trick laughed softly and shook his head. "And I'm an idiot, sitting here with everything I want and trying to convince you to not take me back!"

"And I was a bastard who didn't tell you all the truth, so we even up." Bast nuzzled against Trick's hand, nibbling on the salt-sweet fingers as they passed. "We're together now, that's the cool part."

Trick grinned at him and brought the fingers back to his lips. "Yeah, that's pretty cool."

Bast slid his lips over two of Trick's fingers, sucking and licking. A soft, happy noise built in his chest as Trick's flavor filled his mouth.

"Oh..." Trick pressed closer and leaned down, licking at Bast's lips around his own fingers. "I think I'm hungrier for your touch than food."

He reached out, stroking Trick's stomach through the t-shirt, working his way up to tease the sweet nipples through the cloth. Bast let his body curl around Trick with a purr, warm and strong. Trick moaned and pressed closer.

He let Trick's fingers go and fastened their lips together, tongue pressing deep into Trick's mouth.

Fuck, his Sweets tasted so good.

Trick pushed him back down onto the bed, rolling with him until he was lying beneath his Sweets' weight. He could feel Trick's need, hard and hot against him.

He tugged at Trick's t-shirt, needing skin and heat and life all around him. Trick sat back, straddling his thighs as his Sweets took off his t-shirt. His own shirt was next, Trick's fingers working the buttons loose.

"You make me so fucking hot."

"Mm... and you make me ache, make me hungry." He reached for Trick, fingers luxuriating in the warm, smooth skin.

Trick pulled him up enough to get his shirt off him, throwing it in the same direction Trick's t-shirt had flown. Bast worked open Trick's jeans, fingers searching for that sweet, hard cock. The back of his hands rubbed against the blond curls, soft and silky.

"Oh, fuck!" Trick shook and pushed into his hand.

"Mm... so hot." Bast wrapped his hands around Trick's cock, pulling easily, loving the heat and silken feel of his Sweets against his fingers.

Making a soft noise, Trick started to rock, rolling into his strokes. Every time his Sweets rolled back, his ass would slide against

Bast's cock, trapped in his trousers. His lips opened -- panting, hungry, needy -- and his thighs parted.

"Bast... want to be naked." Trick's voice was needy, pleading.

"Naked is good. I like naked." He wasn't sure how Trick was going to manage it with him pumping the hard cock, but his Sweets was a bright boy.

Trick was still rocking into his hand, moaning and gasping, pure pleasure on his face.

"In my mouth, Sweets? Up here, take my mouth."

Trick's moans grew louder and he surged up, eager and clumsy and shaking. "Please, yes."

He groaned, head lifting and lips wrapping around the head of Trick's cock.

Trick whimpered and tilted, pushing his cock in deep as he leaned forward and grabbed the headboard. "Shit, Bast... I can't..." Then his hips starting rocking, pushing the hot cock in and out of Bast's mouth.

Bast pushed Trick's jeans down further, hands wrapping around the sweet ass and pulling Trick deeper. Oh, yes. He needed this, wanted this, loved this. Loved Trick.

Trick fucked his mouth, slowly at first, but faster and harder as he didn't protest. He licked and swallowed with each thrust, his own shaft throbbing and needy. His groan, sharp and harsh, vibrated around Trick's cock.

Whimpering, Trick started to jerk gracelessly into his mouth. Sucking hard, he reached up and twisted Trick's nipples, tugging his Sweets over the edge.

"Bast!" Trick shoved deep and came, long pulses of seed filling Bast's belly.

His fingers slid over Trick's body, stroking softly as he sucked, loving Trick with his lips and tongue.

Trick groaned and he could feel the muscles in his Sweets' thighs start to tremble. "Gotta lie down."

Bast flipped him and settled him down on the mattress, worrying at Trick's pale cheeks. "Let me mix you up a protein drink until the food gets here."

If he'd had the slightest bit of sense he wouldn't have fed from Trick, wouldn't have weakened him. *That's it, Sebastian old man,* he thought, *you're officially obsessed.*

He pulled Trick's jeans off and then covered his lover up. "Chocolate or vanilla?"

Trick's hand slid out, grabbing hold of his thigh. "How about a Bast flavored one? Come here and let me return the favor."

"Oh, Sweets..." He shivered, reaching for Trick's face. "Don't tempt me."

Trick smiled and nuzzled into his hand. "But I want to tempt you. Come on, Bast." Trick's hand slid up, moving over his ass. "Don't you want me to suck you?"

"Oh, fuck, yes, but you need nourishment, food, protein." His voice had faded into a whisper, shivering. Fuck, he wanted Trick. Needed him.

"But that's the idea -- there's protein in come, you know."

He groaned, crawling back onto the bed, eyes fastened on Trick's.

"That's right, bring me that feast, baby-boy." Trick's eyes were glittering, hungry and he licked his lips.

Bast popped the button on his slacks, cock immediately pushing free, fascinated by his Sweets' gaze.

"Oh, yeah." Hands wrapping around his ass and tugging him close, Trick looked up at him. "You know, I used to hate doing this -- fastest damn way to make a buck, but, fuck, you feel like a piece of crap doing it. But I don't hate doing it for you."

"No? Because we don't have to." Bast was panting, balls aching and tight.

"No, I want to -- you don't make me feel like a whore for doing it."

Bast reached for his Sweets. "You're not a whore, Trick. You're my lover, my friend. My Sweets."

"Then let your lover suck you off, Bast. Bring me that thing before one of us gets poked in the eye with it."

"We can't have that." Bast chuckled and scooted away, pushing off his slacks and leaning forward for a kiss, nibbling at Trick's bottom lip.

Trick moaned and his tongue slid out, softly meeting Bast's. Bast whimpered, sliding close so their bodies pressed together as they kissed. Hot and soft and slow and closer to perfect than anything had the right to be, their tongues and lips touched. Not explored, not fucked, not aroused -- *touched.*

Trick's hands came up, moving into his hair, his Sweets making a soft sound. His own fingers copied Trick's caresses, stroking through the shaggy, thick hair, massaging Trick's scalp, loving his Sweets, touching and holding the warm, beloved body.

The warm fingers slid down to his neck, tickling and stroking. Bast's fingers followed Trick's -- continuing down to play over the warm chest and belly and then farther still, tangling in the wiry curls growing in the hollow of Trick's hips.

"Bast..." Trick groaned and undulated beneath him.

"Mm... Sweets." Bast met Trick's dazed eyes, half-drunk on passion himself. "So good."

Trick's hands slid down along his sides and met beneath him, sliding against his cock.

"Nothing like your touch, Sweets. I've ached for it, for the touch of your hands." Bast nibbled on the soft flesh beneath Trick's ear, licking and sucking with gentle hunger.

Trick gasped and his hands turned, closing over Bast's cock, working it slowly.

"Trick, oh, yes. Please. Touch me." His hips rocked into the touch, steady and easy, need rippling inside him, the pulse of Trick's heart under his lips.

Trick's fingers tightened, sped, slid over his cock like need and desire made flesh.

All of a sudden they rolled, Trick pressing him into the mattress, mouth covering his for a single hot kiss before his Sweets slid down his body and began to nuzzle his erection.

"Oh, Sweets..." Bast stretched out, shifting on the bed, encouraging the touch of hand and tongue and lips.

Trick took his time, licking his straining flesh from top to bottom and up again. The sweet tongue slid into the tip, Trick groaning at the taste.

He needed. Oh, fuck, he needed.

He could hear the pounding of Trick's heart in his head, his lover's beat driving him, sending him soaring.

Trick took the head of his cock into his mouth and sucked hard, head bobbing as he took Bast in completely. A moment later Trick's mouth was gone again, his Sweets licking at his balls and pulling them into that hot mouth, loving them completely.

"Trick! Fuck!" He spread his legs, cradling Trick's heat, the sensation of warmth pushing him just that much higher.

That sweet tongue explored him, slick against the soft skin beyond his balls and then againsthis opening. A few urgent pushes slid the tip into him and then Trick moaned and shifted, swallowing him down again. This time his Sweets' head bobbed, up and down, over and over, taking him in deep.

Bast twisted, arching up into the sucking heat again and again, the throb of their passion ringing inside him. "Oh, Sweets. Sweets! Gonna come. Gonna... oh..."

He stiffened and came, seed filling his Sweets' mouth in steady pulses. Trick drank him down and then began to lick him, tongue moving over his cock until it was soft.

Bast was floating, little purrs filling the air, body shifting on the bed. "Good. So good."

Trick slowly kissed his way up to Bast's mouth, filling it with Trick's tongue and his own flavor.

He curled close, falling headlong into Trick's presence. "This is real, right? I'm really home with you?"

"God, I hope so." Trick nuzzled against him, soft kisses landing randomly over the skin of his neck and shoulders.

"Oh, me too, Sweets. Me, too."

He held his Sweets tight, face buried in the softness of the heavy-silk hair. Trick's hands moved over his skin, stroking him. The motions slowed, faded, and then stopped altogether, Trick murmuring something soft and sleepy sounding.

Bast's eyes focused up at the painting. He looked beyond the paint, beyond the still stones, seeing the gentle, most beloved eyes of the long-dead man who'd painted it for him, smiling at him, worry eased.

"I'm home again and happy. Rest."

He closed his eyes, pulling the blankets around them, snuggling, and taking his own advice.

Chapter Eight

"Sebastian?" The voice was low, husky and weak, and it still hurt to hear it, even after all this time, tiny metal hooks under his skin, the splash of full sun on naked skin.

He watched his hands as they wrung out a lace-edged cloth, brought it over to flatten across Bryce's forehead, once smooth and golden, now marred and grey, like the sparse hair that fell upon the pillow. "Yes, my love, I'm here."

Oh, gods, here again. Not here again. Not watching again.

Eyes that couldn't see him, hadn't seen him in months, rolled, lost. Sebastian -- not yet Bast, not here in this brocade-and-velvet-draped sickroom, not with the clatter and stench of London just outside, just downstairs -- traced a hand down his lover's chest, wincing at the death he felt there, at the pang of loss blooming fresh in his own heart.

"Bryce, oh, love. Let me help you. Let me save you..."

He hated the need echoing in his voice, hollow, empty. Hated the flat rank humanity of it.

Bryce shook his head, a cough wracking the too-thin body, lips taking on a blue tint, as if he had been nibbling the ends of his brushes again, absently trying to decide whether that piece of sky needed more indigo...

"Please." He didn't recognize his own voice, fury at the gods mingled with the purest agony. "Please, love."

A cold hand touched his cheek, wiped away invisible tears. "No, my sweet boy. I have no wish to share your curse. I would miss the sun, the dawn, the taste of peaches. I have no wish to watch those I love leave me."

"I would never leave you. Never." Sebastian slid to his knees with a sob, trapped here in this moment, holding Bryce's hand in his own. "Am I not enough for you? Not enough to live for?"

"You are, my love, but I am a man. We are not the same."

"We could be. We could be, love." Time was fading for Bryce, the dawn so close and so unforgiving and he knew that the moon would next find him broken and empty. He knew. He always knew. This never changed, no matter how he dreamt it.

So he begged.

"I love you, Sebastian, but I cannot stay, not here, not like this." Another coughing fit, this one harsh and painful, rocked his lover, slamming him into the mattress, not even the down-filled pillows enough to keep the black bruises from staining the fine skin.

From where he sat, he could see the tiny scars left from a lifetime of loving, of feeding, of teasing and pleasure and being whole. Four hundred years he'd waited to find Bryce.

Four hundred years of waiting and the gods were taking his Bryce after a mere forty-two years, three months and fifteen too-short days. Four hundred years of waiting and he could not keep his lover well.

"I would do it again." His whisper was empty. He would do it again. And again.

"I know, my boy. Let me go. I will have my eye upon you always."

With a cry of loss that set the dogs in the courtyard barking, he bit into the thin wrist, taking a last taste, setting his heart and soul free from the pain in the only way he knew how.

He could only hope the flavor under his tongue would last.

Bast woke with a long, low cry, tears flowing, arms open and searching as they had been every night for weeks.

For the first time since he'd started waking from the dreams, he was answered, a soft grumble and warm body pressing close. Trick. He curled in, sobbing in either loss or relief and maybe it was both because Trick's touch eased him, like nothing had and he couldn't imagine what that meant. Didn't want to imagine. Wouldn't.

Trick's arms wrapped around him as his Sweets came fully awake and he was pulled tight against the warm body. "Bast?"

"'m okay. Nightmare. Just a bad dream." He hated it, hated that his Bryce was reduced to a phantasm, a ghost. Hated that those sweet green eyes were nothing more than a watchful memory.

Bast raised his tear-stained face up for a kiss. It was granted immediately, Trick's lips sleep-soft and sloppy.

Oh.

Worry and distress faded and a sweet arousal and hunger filled him instead. He pressed up into the kiss, not pushing and taking, but sharing and thanking and relaxing all at once.

Trick's hands moved over his back with long, soothing strokes. "Better, baby-boy?"

"Yes. Yes. Better." They were pressed together, shoulders to toes -- well, his toes. Trick's were a bit farther than he could reach. He was warm and horny and happy and hungry and home. "Much better."

"Good." Trick nuzzled him, tongue coming out to lick at his skin, sliding over the tracks of his tears.

He chuckled, the soft wetness tickling at him, his hands sliding over Trick's warm, smooth skin. "Yes, good, Sweets."

"You wanna talk about the dream?"

He shook his head. "Bad memories. I've racked a few hundred up, you know?" He pressed closer. "I vote we create some good ones instead."

"I can go with that." Trick's mouth covered his again, this kiss harder, more awake and aware and aroused. Bast groaned, purring into Trick's lips as the addictive music of his sweet's need moved through him. Fuck, he was hungry.

Trick rubbed against him, heat growing hard between them. He arched, pulling his lips away from temptation. No biting. No feeding. Just fucking. Focus, Sebastian! Focus! Trick whimpered, lips following him, searching out his skin.

He rubbed their groins together, heat against heat. "Fuck me, Sweets? Want to ride you. Please."

Trick whimpered again, jerking against him. "Yes. Oh, fuck, yes."

Bast settled Trick back none too gently and straddled him. Without preparation or thought, he pushed himself down onto the thick tip of Trick's cock, trusting in the burn to steal the edge of hunger. Bast hissed and stiffened, slowly working himself down.

Trick's hands slid around his waist, gripping hard. He could feel his Sweets' hips twitching, knew Trick wanted to move, to thrust up into him, but was holding back.

He finally settled, burn fading into sweet ache, Trick filling him. He looked down into blazing eyes, so blue against the velvet. "Take me, Sweets. Give me all you've got."

Bringing his knees up, Trick planted his feet on the mattress and began to buck up, thrusting into him.

He rode Trick hard and fast, pushing his desperation and hunger into the motions, sinking into the delicious feeling of thrusting and sliding and pushing and fucking.

Trick was calling out, voice raised in passion and need, his Sweets' body arching and writhing beneath him.

He was so fucking beautiful, so vital, so alive.

Bast sobbed softly, reaching down to tug his own cock, pulling hard.

One of Trick's hands joined his own, wrapping around his fingers and his cock.

"Sweets. Oh, fuck. Yes, Sweets. Yes." Bast arched backwards, screaming as his balls tightened and seed pulsed over their joined fingers.

Trick surged up into him, cock pulsing and shooting liquid heat into him.

So good. So fucking good. He curled forward with a soft moan, resting his head on Trick's chest.

"Oh, Bast, I've missed you so much." Trick was murmuring softly, hands sliding over his skin. "Missed being warm, missed waking up and making love, missed kissing."

"Yes. I need this. Was dying inside without it." He kissed Trick's sternum, closing his eyes. "Need you."

Trick's hands stuttered, stopped and then slowly began their soft wandering again. "Why me?" Trick asked softly.

"Why not you?" He nuzzled, hands sliding over Trick's skin, slow and easy.

Trick shrugged. "I could probably give you a few reasons, but I told myself if I got a second chance, I wasn't going to blow it again."

"Just trust me? I know what I want." He looked up into Trick's face. "I know who I need."

Trick smiled softly at him. "I can do that."

"Good." Trick's belly rumbled and he grinned. "Breakfast? The groceries should be upstairs."

"Yeah -- I'm starving!"

He pushed off Trick's chest, groaning as their bodies separated. "Gimme a second to clean up and find a robe and I'll go grab the box."

Trick's hands slid over him as he got up. "I'll give you a hand."

He chuckled, his own hunger nipping at him. "With cleaning up, finding a robe, or grabbing the box?"

Trick stretched, skin pulling tight over bones and muscles. "Which do you want help with?"

"Yes, but you need to eat. So I'll take your help with grabbing the box and I'll save luxuriating with you in the shower for after breakfast."

He wandered into the bathroom, wiping himself clean and grabbing two robes from the huge closet.

He needed to call Bael, needed to call Frost and get the blood delivered, needed... Oh, fuck, what he needed was Trick.

"Here's your robe, muscles. Come lug groceries."

Trick laughed and climbed out of bed, coming over to him and grabbing a long kiss.

Once Trick had the robe on, he grabbed Bast around the waist and picked him up, heading toward the elevator. "Muscles?"

"Yes!" Bast crowed, holding onto Trick's shoulders as he teased. "My muscle-bound Sweets."

"Muscle-bound?" Trick laughed, setting Bast down to open the grating. "I'm not sure if that was a compliment or an insult?"

Bast ran his hands over Trick's ass, purring loudly. "A compliment, Sweets, always."

"Cool."

Closing the grating, Trick set the elevator in motion and then pushed him up against the side of it and kissed him.

"Oh..." He wrapped his arms around Trick's neck, hunger filling him again, making him shake.

"What's the matter, baby-boy?"

"Nothing. Just hungry, Sweets." He rested his forehead on Trick's shoulder, snuggling close. "I'll call Frost, see when he can make a delivery. If he can't show, I'll go visit Bael for a snack, yeah?"

Trick raised his head and looked down into his eyes. "It's my fault you're hungry in the first place. If you need to... feed, I'm here."

"I just... you need to eat. You were so weak last night and I don't want to hurt you." Bast closed his eyes. "I don't want to lose you."

Trick's arms wrapped around him. "I'm fine -- nothing a little steak won't take care of."

He wanted so much, just a bite, a nibble. The elevator stopped with a thump, jostling them. "Well, let's... let's get some steak into you and we'll talk."

Trick gave him a grin. "Hey, I'm not gonna push you into sucking my blood -- I just don't want you starving if you don't have to, you know? I know what it's like to be hungry."

Trick stepped out and put the two boxes of groceries into the elevator, pressing the bottom to get them back down again. Trick went through the boxes idly until they stopped moving.

"I thought you didn't eat food? There's enough for an army here."

"You said you were hungry."

"Yeah, I did. I am." Trick stomach growled loudly, agreeing.

"Good." He grinned and went for the phone. "Your food, your kitchen. Put it where you want, Sweets. I'm gonna call Frost and Bael."

"That guy doesn't like me much," Trick told him as he disappeared into the kitchen. "All right! Top cut meat."

"What guy? The grocer?" He grabbed his address book, looking up Frost's number and pulling the phone out of the cabinet.

"No, the black guy." Trick's voice was muffled, mouth full.

"Bael? What hap... hold on." Frost's voice sounded and, quick as he could offer cash, the deliveries were scheduled -- starting tomorrow. "Tomorrow, Frost? Damnit! None today? There's no way? I'll double your money."

Trick came out, plate full of cold chicken and potato salad with a Coke balanced on the edge, and came to sit close.

He rolled his eyes and stole a quick kiss, arguing fruitlessly and finally settling on tomorrow. He hung up the phone with a sigh. "He's *such* an asshole. So? What's up with you and Bael?"

Trick shrugged and looked down at his plate. "We kind of had an argument. Well... I conned him into showing up here and then slammed him against the wall and demanded he tell me where you were. He wasn't forthcoming."

Bast blinked. "Maybe I'll just call before he shows up looking for me. He'll figure out I'm gone eventually and this is the first place he'll come." Looking to kick Trick's ass, probably, convinced that Trick had attacked him.

He blushed and grinned. Trick really wanted to find him.

Really.

"He's not going to be happy you're back with me."

"He'll adjust. No one's forcing him to stick around, Sweets." Bast settled onto the bed. Bael was a good friend, a player. He'd come around.

He dialed up Bael's number and waited for the hello. "Bael, pretty? 's Bast."

"Lover! You sound great, babe. What's up? You want some more sugar?"

"From you, pretty? Always. But, Bael, pretty? There's something I need to tell you. Trick came to see me last night and I came home." He smiled over at Trick.

"What? How the hell did he find you? Oh, babe -- you didn't call him?"

"No. No... he... he found me. He's a smart one, my Trick. He found me and brought me home. I've missed being home, pretty. Missed you and Rose and Bear." Bast lowered his voice. "I... I was so glad to see him, Bael. I needed him. You know that."

"Damn it, Bast -- that boy isn't out for anything more than a meal ticket. He's hurt you once already, he's going to do it again -- next time he might kill you before he leaves you! I'm coming down there. You can kick him out and I'll back you up -- pay him off if you have to, but you have to get rid of him."

"No, no. Come on now, Bael. Trust me, please? I'm not kicking him out. Hell, it's *his* house, pretty! I *want* to stay!" Bast hopped off the bed, stalking back and forth.

"Lover... He's got you blinded. You've been half-dead for months, it nearly killed you when he left, and now you're back with him? Bast..." He could hear the pain and worry in Bael's voice.

"No, Bael. I... I need... wanted to come back. Wanted to try again. Please, pretty, try to understand." He wandered over to the bar and poured himself a scotch. "He knows now, we'll be able to play together -- me and you and Rose and Trick and Bear... we'll dance and party, pretty."

Trick was still eating, watching him.

"You make sure you make that soon, babe. And I'm going to call you twice a day, and if you don't answer, I'm going to come down there."

"It's a deal. I want to introduce you two properly, let you get to know Trick." Bast relaxed, voice warming. "We'll have fun soon, pretty. I just need to get settled."

He had planned on asking Bael for a drink, just to tide him over, but it didn't seem like a good time. He'd just make do until the bags came.

"Very soon, babe."

"Yes, Bael. Very soon. I promise. I need a shower, pretty. I'll call." With that he hung up the phone, sighing. Things were much less complicated when you could just claim a long retreat in the country, please contact my manservant.

"Everything okay?" Trick nudged him with his hip on the way to the kitchen with the empty plate.

"Yeah. Yeah. He's a good friend. He worries."

Bast put the phone away with another sigh. "I'm going to take a shower, Sweets."

He wasn't making a mistake, was he?

It wasn't until he'd managed to get into the hot water, with his shampoo and his soap and steam all around him, that the tension faded from his shoulders.

A few minutes later, Trick slid the door open. "Want some help with your back?"

"Always." He stretched up along the slick black tile, hands rubbing over the rippled texture, offering himself up to sensation. The water poured over his back and ass, almost too hot to bear, and he parted his thighs, letting the water slide over the sensitive skin behind his balls.

He was shielded suddenly from the water, Trick's hands sliding along his back.

So good, better than the water -- and Bast hadn't found much that could be better than the pounding throb on his muscles.

"Sweets."

"Your skin is so soft, smooth." Trick's mouth slid along his shoulder, nibbling and licking.

He let his head fall to one side, humming softly. He'd missed this terribly -- the comfort and sensation of Trick's touch. It echoed inside him, called to him, sang to him.

"I hope you don't mind I'm hogging all the water -- been a while since I had a hot shower." Trick chuckled and pressed close, hands sliding along his arms until they reached his hands. Trick linked their fingers, body moving gently against his own. "In fact, the last one was here. I think we actually managed to soap up that time, too."

"So long, Sweets?" He wriggled back, squeezing his fingers gently. "That's why I left you the warehouse, Trick, so you'd have the basics." Trick would never need anything but him again. He would assure that.

The possessive assurance in that thought startled him, scared him. Trick wasn't his. Trick was free to go. He didn't even *like* needy lovers, possessive friends.

"I didn't want it. I... I wasn't a whore for you before the argument, I didn't want to be after." Trick shrugged and a little bit of space opened between them. "I know it's what I am and if I don't take what I can it's gonna leave me cold and hungry but... I just... I was your lover, not your whore, and I didn't want to lose that."

Bast turned, pressed up against Trick. "You are my lover, Sweets. This isn't about the money. *We're* not about the money."

Trick nodded. "I just wanted to make sure we both knew that."

He looked up at Trick, still and serious. "I know what we are, I know who we are. No bullshit, Sweets."

He was rewarded with a slow, warm smile.

Pushing up, he kissed the corner of Trick's smile, tasting Trick's pleasure. The smile grew, lips parting as they curved upward. Then Trick was kissing him back, tongue warm and lingering along the insides of his lips.

Wrapping his arms around Trick's neck, he pressed close, encouraging the kiss the deepen, reveling in their bodies' touch.

Trick's hands slid down and grabbed his ass, pulling him closer still as that warm tongue pushed in to slide across his own.

"Mm..." Bast rubbed his cock against the slick warmth of Trick's belly, aroused but not desperate. Not yet.

"You taste like a really good steak," Trick whispered against his lips. "Like if I were to bite into you, you'd be all tender, cool, melt-like-butter-in-my-mouth meat, dripping with blood."

"Oh... Oh, fuck, Sweets." Nothing could send him from gentle arousal to sheer fucking desperation like Trick could. He shuddered, growling soft and low.

"You like that, Bast? Like the thought of me eating you up?"

"Makes me hot. Makes me hungry." He nibbled on Trick's bottom lip, body moving against his Sweets, slinky and needy and starving.

Trick purred and pushed him up against the tiles, body sliding hot and urgent against him.

Bast sobbed and whimpered into Trick's lips, tongue searching for the chocolate and whiskey flavor that was his lover. Still pushing rhythmically against him, Trick's mouth opened to him, wide and hot. His Sweets was moaning and purring and rubbing against him like there was no tomorrow.

He crawled up Trick's body, legs wrapping around his Sweets' hips and holding tight.

"Hot... so hot."

Growing more frantic, Trick sped his motions, pulled him tighter against the warm body, pushed him harder against the tile. Bast squeezed, arching and moaning, balls tightening as their cocks slid together.

Trick started to whimper, motions becoming jerky and graceless, his Sweets all but slamming him against the wall. Bast buried his face into Trick's shoulder as he came, lips measuring the quick heartbeat.

With a sound somewhere between a whimper and a shout, Trick came too, heat splashing against his stomach. He kept his eyes closed, swallowed hard against his hunger, and floated on the scent of Trick and him together.

Trick pressed soft kisses against his neck and shoulder and then pulled back. "Come back to bed with me?"

"Yes. Please." He nodded, reaching out to turn off the shower. "Yes."

Trick carried him out and wrapped them in a towel and then took him to bed where they curled into each other.

"You think the sex is always going to be this good, this hot?" Trick asked.

"If it's not in twenty years, we'll go on one of those swinger's cruises." Bast grinned and nuzzled close. "It's good with you, you make me hungry, you make me need."

"Twenty years... wow... I guess that's not a lot for you, but it seems like forever for me -- longer'n I've been alive."

Twenty years was a heartbeat. Forty was only two.

"Does it freak you out more that I'm 750 years old or that I still want to be your lover in twenty years?"

"The seven-hundred-and-fifty-years-old thing? That doesn't really seem real. The other..." Trick shrugged and pushed closer. "I'm used to long term meaning overnight. The thought of you knowing now that you'll still want me in twenty years -- yeah, it freaks me out."

"I kind of like it," Trick added in a whisper.

"Good." Bast stroked Trick's cheek, holding him close. "I kind of like the idea myself."

Trick chuckled suddenly. "750 years... I bet it'll take twenty years just to make a dent in what you know about sex."

"Sweets, it'll take twenty years to go through what my *friends* know about sex." He winked, nipping playfully at Trick's neck.

Trick chuckled, head going back, exposing the sweet line of neck he'd been playing with.

"Fuck, you're showing a feast to a starving man there, Sweets." He nuzzled, licking and nibbling on the fine, salty skin.

"You hungry?" Trick's fingers traced his lips. "Do you need... do you need me?"

"Please, don't. I'm trying to be good." His tongue slipped out, tasted the tip of Trick's finger. "Trying really hard."

"I don't want you to be hungry."

"I've been hungry for weeks. One more day won't make a difference." Bast closed his eyes, the hunger within them making them glow.

"Oh... open your eyes -- let me see. Please?"

Bast looked up, his black eyes glowing a soft green, his hunger obvious in the line of his face, the instinctive seduction of his body.

A trembling hand reached out and slid through the hair on his head. "I didn't notice how beautiful you were like this."

He purred softly, arching into the touch. It fed his need and sparked his hunger all at once.

"What's it feel like?"

"What? The hunger or the feeding?" His voice rasped, low and rich, and he luxuriated in not hiding his face, just relaxing into the pulse of blood and passion.

Trick's fingers were back at his mouth, tracing his lips. "Oh. Both, I guess."

"The hunger's like needing an orgasm, right before you come, when your balls are aching and you're *just* there." He opened his lips, let Trick touch the sharpness of his fangs. "The feeding is better."

Trick's finger's slid along his teeth. "So you're hurting."

"Yeah, but it's tolerable. I'm a big guy." Trick's finger caught on his fang, he could see the flash of shocked pleasure in his Sweets' eyes. He licked the blood away and healed the wound in one motion. "Fuck... so good."

"Oh!" Trick's hips pushed against him, cock hard, breath coming quickly. "That was..."

"Yeah. I told you. No pain, just pleasure." He snuggled close, growling. "One day, if you want, I'll feed while I'm sucking you off. It'll blow your mind."

"Oh, fuck." Trick rolled his hips again, sliding his cock along Bast's belly. "What are you going to do today?"

"Let me taste you? I'm so hungry for you, need you, Sweets." He curled around Trick, nibbling and stroking. So hungry, he was so fucking hungry.

Trick nodded, rubbing against him. "Yes." His Sweets was breathless, voice low, husky.

"You sure?" He licked a line over the sweetly pulsing vein, almost sobbing, body moving faster. "Tell me you're sure."

Trick's body matched his, there was need in the blue eyes, sharp and strong. "I'm sure."

"Oh, Trick..." He nuzzled close, plastering his body to Trick's. He struck quick and deep, mouth filling with the dark, rich heat of blood.

Trick's scream echoed around the room, heat splashed against his stomach as blood pulsed into his mouth.

He shuddered, drinking with long, strong pulls. His cock was full, rubbing against Trick frenetically. Moon above, he needed this. Needed this so fucking bad.

Bast came as his stomach filled. He gasped, hips jerking with aftershocks as he closed the wound, licking Trick's throat with a long, slow motion.

Trick was trembling in his arms, eyes wide and stunned.

"You okay, Sweets? You doing okay?" He dropped soft kisses over Trick's face, stroking him gently.

"I just didn't expect. Wow. I mean. It was... like I was inside you."

Trick curled into him. "Don't let go," whispered his Sweets.

"No, I'm right here." He snuggled, touching and kissing, whispering stories of his childhood, his past. Bast kept the world away, let Trick fall back into himself easy and safe.

Eventually the touches were returned, Trick nuzzling close. "That was the most incredible thing I have ever felt."

Bast took a kiss, sated and full and surfeited. "Thank you. I needed you, needed a taste of you."

"Do people taste different? I mean... well, blood is blood, isn't it?"

"Fuck no! I mean, that shit in the bags? McDonald's, you know? No flavor, nothing but calories and a full belly. But fresh blood? Everybody's different -- what they eat, how they live, who they are. It's all different."

He grinned at Trick. "Like you, Sweets? Dark and rich and fucking addictive. Good ninety-dollar whiskey with a hint of dark chocolate and a whisper of roasted coffee."

Trick chuckled. "I taste like all that?"

Bast nodded. Like that and more, deeper, something that made his fucking balls ache and had since the very start, but he wasn't going to mention that part, was he?

"You're addictive."

Trick's cheeks reddened. "You're kinda addictive yourself, Bast. I couldn't stay away no matter how much I thought it would be a good idea."

"I'm glad you couldn't, Sweets."

"Yeah, me too."

Trick snuggled closer, eyes beginning to drift shut. "Don't know why 'm so tired..."

"Been a stressful few days and you've not been taking care of my Sweets." Bast tugged the heavy coverlet over them both, well and truly full for the first time in too long. "We're safe here. *Home* here."

"Been a long time since I had a home," Trick told him, sounding like he was already half asleep. "Never really missed it 'til now."

"It's real now, Sweets. You're home, I'm home." Bast found his place on Trick's shoulder and settled down, lips finding Trick's pulse as he closed his eyes.

It beat strong and steady, slowly filling him with peace.

Chapter Nine

"Bael, pretty... I'm *fine*. Honestly! I'm having a glorious time relaxing and working." Bast wandered around the apartment, hips moving to the music, waiting for Trick to get home from... wherever he'd said he was going. Possibly to speak with the warehouse manager.

Trick had taken quite the interest in his new acquisition. It was quite adorable, really.

What wasn't adorable was Bael's constant fucking worry. It was getting boring.

"Look, pretty, I have to run. Email's bouncing in from all over. I'll try to get out this week and go dancing."

"Tonight, babe?" Bast frowned; there was almost desperation in the southern drawl.

"No. I'm not dressed for dancing." He looked down at his faded blue jeans and pirates-of-the-Caribbean knock off that he'd been wearing to screw around the apartment. "Not a chance. How about coming for a drink or three on Friday night?"

He was pretty sure he could talk Trick into that and Bast knew, once they relaxed, Bael and Trick would get along fabulously.

"At your place? Your... Trick won't mind?"

"No, he'll be fine." That did the trick and got him off the fucking phone before he threatened to tear the throat out of one of the best friends he had.

He turned up the music and closed his eyes, swaying to the heavy, driving beat, letting it relax him.

A couple of songs later and the elevator began to groan.

Oh, perfect. He turned the music into something throbbing and sheer sex and untied his shirt. He moved to the middle of the room, hips picking up the rhythm and undulating before the elevator grate opened.

"Holy fuck! I'm gonna go away more often if this is what I'm coming back to." Trick's eyes burned, his Sweets stalking toward him.

Nothing like being stalked by his Sweets. He moved slower, tempting, broadcasting his desire.

"Oh yeah..." Trick's body started to mimic his and by the time Trick's hips pressed against him, they were moving in perfect sync.

"Hey, Sweets. Missed you." Bast groaned, sliding against Trick's heat, arms wrapping over strong shoulders.

Trick's hands met on his buttocks, pulling him tight against the rocking hips. "Missed you, too. Feels like I was gone forever."

He lifted his face, Trick's smiling lips meeting his in a melting kiss that intensified the music, the pulsing beat.

Wrapping him tight and close, Trick devoured his mouth, his Sweets hungry.

Oh.

Bast melted with a low, happy purr. His bared belly rubbed against the softness of Trick's t-shirt, the simple silver belt buckle a cool contrast.

He could feel the heat of Trick's cock, hard against him. His Sweets gave a low moan and began biting at his lips.

Oh, so nice. So *hungry*. Bast wondered for a breath what his Sweets had seen to get so fucking turned on. Of course, asking meant no more sweet bites.

He'd ask later.

Trick was walking him backwards, only stopping when they hit a piece of furniture. It turned out to be the divan, which was just as well as they fell onto it together, Trick between his spread legs. Bast wrapped around Trick's heat, arms and legs, hips pushing up against him, driving with the music.

Gasping, Trick moved with him, teeth still nipping his skin. "Are you hungry?"

"For you, Sweets? Always." He gave a little chuckle that turned into a gasp. Yanking at Trick's shirt, he searched for skin. "You want to fuck me? Take me hard?"

"Oh, yeah - that would be good, too." A soft shudder went through Trick. "Want to be inside you when... do you want to feed, baby-boy?"

"Trick..." His hunger flared, hot and wild and feral. His eyelids lowered, face nuzzling against Trick's shoulder, as he hid. "Make me ache, wanting you."

"Don't." Trick's body was still moving urgently against him, one hand coming up to tilt his face. "Please don't hide from me. Want to see you. Need to feel you, to be inside you."

"Oh, fuck." He met Trick's eyes fully, intensity flaring in the pit of his stomach. He turned his head, nipping sharp against Trick's wrist, tongue lapping the tiny drops, growling low. "So sweet. Want you, Trick. Need you."

Trick shuddered against him, hips pressing harder, closer. "Yes, please, Bast. Want you to feed, baby-boy."

"Yes." He tilted Trick's head, licking at the sweet skin that would one day hold his marks permanently. "Now, Sweets." With that he bit, world going red.

Screaming, Trick jerked against him. He could feel Trick's heartbeat pushing the blood into his mouth, could hear his Sweets' breath as if it were his own.

Trick's need tasted sharp, sweet and necessary beneath his tongue, and he didn't take much -- only enough to settle the balance between them, to fill the hole within him with Trick's blood.

Trick shuddered and shook and held on tight, soft whimpers falling from his mouth, breath hot against Bast's skin. Bast lapped the remaining salt-copper-honey-hot drops as the wound closed, faded into little pink memories.

With a small gasp, Trick's body stilled, heavy and solid against him. "Oh, man, I could get used to that."

Bast chuckled, nuzzling and tickling. "Like that, do you, Sweets?"

"Just a little." Trick grinned against his skin and then tasted him with a warm, wet tongue.

"Mmm... are you hungry now, my lovely one?" Sated now, he could hear the lazy, sensual purr in his voice, tempting his lover to stay and play.

"Oh yeah." Trick chuckled. "Maybe in the shower? My jeans are a mess."

"The shower is my second home, Sweets." Bast's hands finally worked Trick's t-shirt free and he pulled it up, exposing the tiny, hard nipples. "Ooh... if we're going to move, let's go. Those are tempting."

Trick laughed and took his mouth again, the happy sound pushing into him along with Trick's tongue.

He could taste Trick's pleasure, and he opened to the kiss, hungry for more.

It was Trick who broke the kiss, making a face and wriggling off him and pulling at the black jeans. "Shower, before I become attached down here."

Grinning, Bast shrugged off his shirt and unfastened the top button of his jeans. Oh, yeah, shower sex was the best and led to naked in-bed cuddling and late night monster movie marathons and popcorn-and-jellybean flavored kisses.

Trick was already out of his clothes, tossing them toward the dresser as he sprinted for the bathroom. "I'm gonna get in the shower before you, Bast!" Trick crowed. "You're starting to slow down."

"Hey! Give an old man a break!" He shimmied out of his jeans and headed toward the shower.

"You sure didn't feel like an old man a minute ago!"

"No? You sure?" He grabbed Trick's ass, pinching it hard enough to sting.

Trick yelped and turned, pushing him up against the tiles. "Oh, you're in trouble now!"

Bast squeaked and struggled -- well, not really, but he liked to play fair and he *loved* the way Trick hunted -- sliding on the wet tile.

Trick got him turned around, knees spreading his legs, and one of Trick's fingers found its way into his opening, pushing deep. "I've got you now, Bast."

"Ooh..." He pressed back, riding Trick's finger. "What're going to do with me?"

"I was thinking I'd fuck you up against the wall." A second finger joined the first inside him.

Bast widened his stance, humming, eyes falling closed as he flew. "Good plan."

"I'm glad you approve," murmured Trick, running his teeth along Bast's shoulder and neck.

"Oh fuck!" Bast's head fell forward, body tightening at the flash of sensation.

"You like that? You like it when I bite you back?"

"Yes." His answer was captured by the water, pleasure and need twining in the base of his spine.

"Oh..." The sounds was half groan, half growl and Trick was spreading his ass cheeks and pushing into him, cock hard and wet.

His Sweets' teeth sank into his neck, not quite hard enough to break the skin. His strangled scream echoed, bouncing off the black tile, and his cock throbbed, so full, so hard.

"Oh, God, I love making you scream." Trick started to thrust into him, long, hard lunges that were accompanied by bites all along his throat.

Bast was flying, almost as high as feeding, the harsh, burning pressure delicious and perfect, driving him towards pleasure. One of Trick's hands slid around to his cock, grabbing it roughly and pulling hard.

"Show me how much you love it. Show me."

"Fuck! Sweets! Yes!" He ground back against Trick's cock and screamed, cock pulsing hot and hard in the strong hand.

Trick went back to fucking him, his Sweets' breath hot in his ear, the cry loud as Trick came.

His leaned his head against the tile, shudders running through him. "Trick... oh... fuck."

Trick pressed heavily against him. "Yeah, that was pretty much the idea."

"Wow. You need to meet Rose. You'll rock her world." Bast arched into Trick. "That was... wow."

Trick's arms wrapped around his middle and his Sweets turned him into the spray of water. "The only world I care about rocking is yours," Trick murmured against the top of his spine.

"Oh, good." Bast sank into the kisses and the water, body relaxing completely.

Trick had him soaped up and rinsed in short order and then just stood there for the longest time, supporting him while he stood in the hot spray.

When he could, Bast turned, reaching up to work shampoo into Trick's hair. His fingers massaged Trick's scalp, washing and loving all in one motion.

Trick's eyes closed and he swayed slightly. "Oh, that's nice."

"Yeah. Like touching you." He kissed beneath Trick's jaw. "Like being with you."

"Mm." Trick's arms looped behind his back, holding him easily. Bast closed his eyes and sank into the warm familiarity of Trick's arms.

They stood together for a while longer and then Trick nuzzled him gently. "How about we go to bed and hold each other until night?"

"Mm... yes, Sweets." He was getting lazy, luxuriating in the long, dozy hours wrapped in his Sweets' arms, talking or sleeping or just relaxing.

"Cool."

Trick turned off the water and then wrapped him in a towel, giving himself a quick dry before picking Bast up and carrying him to the bed. It was quickly becoming routine.

They settled together, warm and damp. Bast sighed and ran his hands through Trick's hair, feeding on the contact between them. Trick nuzzled into his touch.

"You're spoiling me. I could get used to this." He gave Trick a soft, lazy kiss, closing his eyes.

"I thought that was the point? Getting used to it, I mean. You said something about twenty years..."

"Twenty years is just the beginning. Barring catastrophe, I'll get to hold you for sixty, at least."

"You're still gonna want me when I'm old and wrinkly and gross?" Trick laughed. "You'll have found someone cuter and younger by then."

"Oh, I'll want you." He flushed and cuddled close. "I'm not as faithless and flighty as I seem."

Trick's hands slid softly against his skin. "Didn't mean that," whispered his Sweets.

"I... it's been a very long time since I found someone to spend a lifetime with. I mean, I play with Bael and Rose -- you know, the lead singer of the Toxics? -- she loves to play with her husband. But that's playing." He hugged Trick tight. "I'm not playing with you."

Trick looked at him for a long moment and then smiled softly. "You know, for once I think I'm just gonna take that at face value."

Bast kissed that smile and then settled down, cheek on Trick's shoulder.

Trick held him close and warm, another thing that was becoming routine. He thought it would be just fine to get used to this.

***

Trick was used to being up most of the night and sleeping at least the morning away, but now he was growing used to sleeping the entire day away, to never seeing the sun.

He couldn't say he missed it that much -- the shine of the moon and the glow in Bast's eyes when he was hungry, when he fed, they were becoming enough to take its place.

He'd just finished a steak, letting Bast lick the blood from the corners of his mouth, when the elevator started groaning.

He frowned at Bast, "You expecting anyone?"

Bast blinked and jerked. "Oh, fuck! What's today? Friday?"

At Trick's nod, Bast shook his head and rolled his eyes. "Fuck, I'm sorry, Trick. I told Bael to come down for some drinks on Friday and lost track of time. You want me to get rid of him, Sweets?"

He shrugged, not sure what Bast wanted him to do. "He doesn't like me, but if you wanted to hang with him I could take off -- I know where I can find a bed for the night, specially if I bring a pizza or something." He tried very hard to keep his voice neutral.

Bast's look was utterly horrified. "Leave? Sweets? No! I was hoping we all could be friends, but if you don't want to, he can leave." A cool hand squeezed his own. "This is *our* home, Trick. Ours."

Relief flooded through him and he squeezed Bast's hand back. "Well, if you think he can refrain from accusing me of being low rent, I can probably put up with him for a drink or two."

He was given a smile and a soft kiss. "I promise -- one tacky comment and he's gone."

The elevator hit the ground floor and the grate rose, Bael sauntering in with a lazy, sensual smile. "Hey there, babe. Trick. I hear there's a vodka and tonic here with my name on it."

"I've got it -- you want something, baby-boy?" Trick asked, watching the black man warily.

"Mmm... whatever you're having, Sweets." Bast lifted his face for Bael's kiss and then Bael settled in the red velvet chair.

He made Bael's vodka and tonic and then poured himself and Bast each two fingers of whiskey.

Bast curled up next to him, thanking him with a soft purr. "It's good to see you, pretty. Been busy? Working hard?"

Trick slid his arm around Bast's shoulders and tried not to look too smug.

Bael nodded, curling up in the chair. "Busy. Been missing you. Rose and the boys say you haven't been out for a show in months. Do you not dance, Trick?"

Trick looked for a hint of anger, but Bael seemed to be honestly asking.

"Yeah, I dance." He smiled at Bast -- they danced all the time, bodies moving sensuously to the beat of whatever was playing.

"Like a fucking dream." Bast gave him a kiss and then grinned at Bael. "You know how I feel about dancers, huh, pretty?"

Trick found himself blushing and he buried his face in Bast's neck as Bael laughed, the sound deep, almost seductive.

"Oh, he is pretty, babe. And you say he dances?" Warm and admiring, the soft drawl felt good.

"Yes, Bael. He dances. He's warm. He's got a sweet stomach and a lovely, delectable ass, too." Bast's hand stroked his shoulder, petting. "Fix yourself another drink, pretty, and tell us what we've been missing."

Trick downed his while Bael was up and asked for another. The big man's fingers lingered as he took the glass and Trick felt his eyebrows rise. He looked at Bast.

Bast grinned. "Bael likes to play, Sweets. No stress. No one's pushing, he's just offering." Bast chuckled, the sound low and throaty. "Think of it as a joint apology and welcome."

Bael handed Trick his whiskey and then moved over to the stereo. "Brought a demo of the Toxics' newest stuff. Wanna?"

Bast crowed and then the room was awash in driving music, the lyrics loud and furious, dark and almost hungry. He could hear why Bast liked them. Bael settled on the arm of the divan, chattering and gossiping about the club kids and Rose and Bear and the Toxics.

Trick sipped at his whiskey, half listening, half watching Bast and Bael flirt with each other. And him. It wasn't direct, but they were definitely including him.

He was starting to react to the combined gazes, and he shifted, spreading his legs to accommodate his cock.

Bast grinned and curled up in his lap, kissing his jaw. "Just making room for Bael, Sweets. He *can't* be comfortable."

"No, the only thing that arm is comfortable for is bending over while you're getting fucked."

He was going to blush again, he just knew it, so he closed his lips over Bast's.

Bast chuckled into his lips, thin arms wrapping around his neck. Trick could hear Bael's throaty laugh, "Yes, this sofa's seen *lots* of action, Trick honey."

"Must be sturdier than it looks."

"Lots of things around here are sturdier than they look, Sweets."

"Oh yeah, I've already figured that out for myself." He grinned over at Bael and gave Bast another quick, hard kiss.

Bast was melting, groaning and purring in his lap. Bael leaned close, lips brushing Bast's cheek. "Can I have a taste? Those lips look good, Trick."

"Of me?" He was surprised -- he'd assumed Bael would want to play with Bast or with him, not with Bast *and* him.

"Mm-hmm. Just a taste. Bast is a patient boy, he can wait." There was obviously a joke there, Bast snorting and nipping Bael's throat playfully. "Let's make up and be friends, Trick."

"Okay, sure."

It wasn't what he'd been expecting, but he was more than willing to go with it. To be more than just Bast's piece of ass, not that he thought Bast thought that, but Bast's friends...

His thoughts were derailed as warm, sure lips closed over his. Bael didn't push, just tasted, slow and easy. His breath smelled like the limes in the vodka and his lips were soft and sensuous.

Bast's slight weight was familiar in his lap, lips nibbling along his collarbone.

He wrapped his arms around Bast, fingers sliding along prominent ribs and opened is mouth, inviting Bael to deepen the kiss.

Bael moaned into his mouth, kiss slowly becoming passionate as their tongues slid together. Bast's body undulated against his hand, wanting and hot.

He was surprised by the ease with which they all moved together. He'd done one or two johns who wanted threesomes and it was always awkward and ungraceful, but with Bast moving in his arms it couldn't be anything but wonderful.

Bael's lips moved away to be replaced by Bast's, his lover's kiss sharper, deeper, edged with a familiar hunger.

Bael stayed close, his lime-sweet breath sliding into their kiss.

He slid his hand down Bast's back, movement stuttering as he found Bael's hand already in the small of Bast's back, shirt pulled up. He froze for half a breath and then let his fingers wander up the long arm. Bael's skin was warm and not quite as soft as Bast's.

Bael's lips wandered to his cheek, brushing and tickling. "Hand feels good, Trick. You must drive Bast to distraction."

Bast chuckled, sensual and happy, into his mouth.

He swallowed the sounds Bast was making, adding happy ones of his own as he relaxed and let himself go, let himself feel.

Bael's lips continued to move, finding his earlobe and sucking. Trick could feel Bael's hand beneath Bast's shirt, teasing the hard little nipples, making Bast gasp and twist in his lap.

He managed to undo a couple of Bael's buttons and slid his hand in, searching for Bael's nipples and offering them the same treatment once he found them.

"Oh!" The word slid from surprised into sexy in a breath, Bael's tongue sliding around his ear.

Bast's fingers were stroking him through his jeans, matching the rhythm of their tongues.

Shit, he wasn't even halfway naked yet and he was ready to go off like a virgin getting it on for the first time.

Bast pushed closer, legs wrapping around his waist, Bael following close behind, pressing against Bast's back.

Bast began to nibble along his jaw and neck, so he turned, searching for Bael's lips, moaning as they found him.

Bast's fingers began working open his shirt, sharp little teeth giving him tiny bites all the way to one of nipples.

Whimpering, he began to thrust with his hips, rubbing up against Bast's hardness. When Bast's teeth closed around his nipple he cried out into Bael's mouth and came, body jerking helplessly against Bast.

Bast purred, lapping his nipples gently as he relaxed back into the cushions.

Bael's lips left his, dark eyes staring at Bast. "Hungry, babe?"

When Bael's head lifted, the long neck was stretched out. Trick could see a hint of scars on the black coffee skin. "Take what you need, babe."

Bast groaned, hunger changing those dark eyes, body reaching toward Bael.

Trick's hands slid around Bast's waist and held on tight, making sure he was a part of this. He wanted to pull Bast to him, could feel the growl building in his belly, and he forced himself to let go.

He leaned forward and took Bael's mouth moments before Bast's teeth sank into the long neck.

Bael groaned, harsh and low, into his lips, body jerking as Bast fed.

Trick broke the kiss burying his head against Bast's shoulder, hands growing tighter and tighter around the trim waist. He wanted it over. He didn't want to have to see this happening again. Ever.

Bast fed for a short time, the act quiet except for Bael's gasps. Trick watched and as soon as Bast drew back, tongue sliding over the wounds, healing them, he took Bast's mouth, pushing his tongue in deep.

Bast purred, hands burying in his hair, lips opening to him. Bast tasted different, not exactly like a merging of him and Bael, but that was the closest he could come to describing it. He swept his tongue through the hot mouth, trying to clear away the unfamiliar taste.

Snuggling close, Bast whimpered into his kiss. His lover's cock was hard, hot against his belly, Bast thrusting against him.

He slid one hand down to Bast's ass, pulling him closer. The other pushed into the tight pants Bast wore, circling the hard flesh.

Bast cried out, arching close. "Trick! Sweets!"

He didn't even care that Bael's hands were cupping Bast's ass as well, he even leaned forward and took the big man's mouth again. It was his name Bast had called, his hand Bast was humping.

Bast groaned, gripping his shoulders hard, coming hard, heat splashing over his hand.

He licked at Bael's lips and then brought his hand up to his mouth, meeting Bast's passion-drugged eyes as he licked the come from his fingers.

"Oh..." Bast surged against him, spent cock jerking. "Sweets."

He chuckled happily and held out his hand. "Want some?"

A hot pink tongue attacked his hand, licking and sucking, soon joined by Bael's hungry lips.

His laughter turned to moans as they sucked his hand, his cock coming back to life.

Bast lifted his head, grinning. "Does this mean you two have made friends?"

Trick met Bael's eyes above his fingers. The black man did something with his tongue that had his toes curling. "Oh yeah..."

"Good boys." A low, sexy chuckle filled the air. "Let's go get a little more naked and a little more friendly, shall we?"

"You just want more Bast sandwich," Trick teased.

"Best thing on the menu, Sweets." Bast winked and bolted for the bed, clothes flying behind him.

"Best not keep him waiting," drawled Bael, standing himself and pulling off his clothing.

Bael was beautiful, strong and lean like a statue from the back, back muscles drawing the eye down to the rounded swells of ass. Compared with Bast's snow-white skin and spare form, he was striking.

Trick got up and undressed more slowly, watching as Bael joined Bast on the bed, sliding easily against him. It was obvious they had fucked for a while, Bast slinking and finding one hot spot after another with lazy ease.

He watched for a moment longer and then joined them, kissing the small of Bael's back, using his lips and tongue and teeth. Bast's hand slid around, stroking through his hair, petting him, welcoming him as much as Bael's groan.

He turned his head to nip at the thin wrist, teeth scraping over the blue veins. Bast's gasp was rewarding, the thin hand reaching to stroke his cheek. Nuzzling, he gave Bast's hand another nip and then returned to kissing Bael's warm, dark skin.

Bael arched into him, Bast surging up to take the dark, full lips in a long, hard kiss. He explored the long spine with his mouth, tracing each vertebra with his tongue, mouthing the skin to either side of it, discovering the places along his back that set Bael shuddering.

"Let me touch you, babe?" The question was rumbled low and needy, Bael whimpering into Bast's lips.

Bast chuckled, light and happy, the sound playful and young and very different than the low, needy sounds Trick was used to hearing.

"If Trick's willing to play, I'm always ready, you know that, pretty."

He raised his head and looked at them. Bael's eyes were full of want, Bast's anticipation.

"What have you got in mind?"

"Anything that makes you comfortable, Sweets. Bael is nothing but easy. Sucking, fucking, groping -- so long as it's not just watching, he's a happy man."

Bael chuckled, nipping at Bast's shoulder. "You know me well, babe."

"I've got to admit that I've been admiring this," Trick murmured, hand moving around Bael's hip to slide along his cock.

Bael's thick cock jerked in his hand. "Oh... he *is* a tempting boy, babe. Fuck, yes. Anything you want."

Bast gave another chuckle and those dark eyes flashed over at him, full of playful amusement.

"How do you want it, baby-boy?" Trick asked.

"I want to suck you, Sweets. You make me hungry." Bast grinned at them. "I could take you both for a ride?"

"At the same time?" His eyes lit up, he could imagine that black cock disappearing into that sweet ass.

"Oh, he likes that, babe." Bael purred, desire evident in every move. "He likes that."

Bast grinned and leaned forward to bite a cherry-dark nipple. "Like you don't, pretty."

Trick laughed, excitement fluttering through him. He leaned forward and took Bael's other nipple in his mouth, attention split between Bael's face and Bast's.

Bast grinned and moved over to nibble his way down Trick's belly, turning every so often to nip at Bael, who was gasping and watching avidly.

Trick reached up and pulled Bael's mouth down, melding their mouths once again. As Bael's tongue pushed inside his mouth, Bast's lips slid over his cock, hot and sucking.

Moaning, he started to fuck Bast's mouth, following the rhythm set by Bael's tongue. He could hear Bast's moan, low and hungry, vibrating around his cock.

Bael's hands slid down, caressing his stomach, the top of Bast's head.

He cleared his throat, swallowing another moan. "Thought you wanted us both at the same time?" Bast knew how fast that got him off.

"Mm... yeah. You want me, pretty?" Bast's lips left him just long enough to ask and then went back to sucking, tongue sliding over his cock.

Bael chuckled and shared a look with Trick. "What do you think, Trick, do you think I want him?"

"How could you not want him?"

Bast stretched out, mouth tightening, and both he and Bael groaned.

Then Bael was moving away, hands black against Bast's pale skin. He watched those hands as they maneuvered Bast's ass into the air, moaning as one long finger disappeared inside Bast. Bast gasped around Trick's cock, thin body shuddering as he rocked back against Bael.

He pushed into Bast's mouth every time Bast rocked back onto Bael, not letting Bast be anything but entirely full or entirely empty.

Bael groaned, one hand pressing against Bast's back. "Want to fuck you, Bast babe."

The mouth around his cock pulled hard, Bast humming and nodding.

Trick moaned. "Oh, I'd put that down as a yes."

Bael lined up with Bast's hole, looking up at Trick with a wolfish grin. "You ready, Trick?"

He could help but return the grin, wondering what it was going to do to Bast's mouth, having that big cock sliding into him. "Bring it on."

Bael pushed inside, a long, slow glide that seemed to go on forever. Bast groaned around his cock, swallowing hard around him, shivering.

"Fuck, he's hot! Nothing like loving you, babe. Nothing." Bael bent forward, kissing Bast's shoulder and Trick's belly before leaning up again.

Trick leaned forward and met Bael's kiss but he soon broke away; he wanted to watch Bast. He wanted to watch that thick black cock slid into Bast's opening. He wanted to watch Bast's mouth as it swallowed his own cock over and over again.

He wanted to watch Bast's body as it undulated between them.

Bael grabbed Bast's hips and began fucking, steady and slow. Bast's mouth slowed, teeth sliding over his cock, sending bolts of lightning up his spine.

He whimpered -- he wanted to come so bad, needed to, but he also wanted the slow, sharp pulls to go on and on forever.

The drags of teeth became sharper as Bael's thrusts grew harder, more desperate. Bast shuddered suddenly, giving a low, broken sound, and the touch of teeth disappeared, becoming fierce, wild pulls.

Trick slid his hand through Bast's shorn hair, wrapping his fingers in what was there as he snapped his hips, pushing hard into Bast's mouth.

He keened softly as he came, pouring his pleasure into his lover. Bast swallowed him down, Bael crying out. "Fuck, tight. Bast! Babe! Fuck!"

Bael jerked into Bast's body, coming with a shuddering cry. Bast lifted his head and sat up, cock hard and bobbing, eyes aglow. He looked from Bael to him, hand moving to his cock. "Need. Hungry."

Trick pushed himself into Bast's arms. "You've already had Bael," he pointed out, covering his own need to be the one.

"Sweets..." Bast's eyes grew brighter, voice low as he pushed Trick to the bed. "Need you."

He spread his arms and his legs wide, tilting his head back, offering all of himself as he whispered, "Then take me."

The cry that slid over his skin was razor-sharp and hungry. Bast panted, hand pumping the thin cock, spreading precome over the tip. "Now? Inside you? Fuck, I can't wait. You ready?"

He grabbed his knees and pulled them further from his body, hips rolling up. "Please, Bast."

Bast moved over him and into him and through him and the room dissolved in a wash of passion and hunger and *fuck* this was Bast's need, pure and real and...

He screamed as he drowned in the pleasure, in the pure rush that was Bast.

When he came to, Bast was curled around him, purring softly, hands sliding over his skin. Soft kisses ranged over his face.

He bided his time, finally turning his head and capturing Bast's lips as they pressed a kiss to the corner of his mouth.

"Trick." Bast kissed him, slow and easy, hands sliding through his hair.

"That was fucking amazing. I think it gets better every time you do it," he whispered, conscious of Bael snuggled up on the other side of Bast.

"Sweets." Bast nibbled his chin, eyes bright and *awake*. "So good."

Suddenly all the questions he'd been ignoring came pushing to the surface and he wanted to know, maybe even needed to know all about it.

He glanced at Bael, wondering when the man was going to go; for some reason he wanted this to be between just him and Bast.

Bast followed his gaze and pressed close, whispering. "Want me to send him home, Sweets? Or we could cuddle on the divan? In the shower? Anything you want."

"I don't want to be rude, but..." he looked into Bast's eyes, letting his lover read his desire, his needs

Bast kissed him and nodded, turning and kissing Bael awake, murmuring. Bael stretched and nuzzled for a second before looking at the clock. "Gotta run, lovelies. Late night party with the twins, you know? Forgive me for fucking and running?"

"Hey, no problem." Trick felt a little bit bad, letting Bael apologize for doing exactly what Trick wanted, but not bad enough to say anything.

Bast chuckled. "We'll plan a nice, long party, pretty. One where you'll have to stay 'til morning."

"Oh, we haven't had a party with all the regulars in a while, babe. Make it happen or I won't be the only one calling looking for you."

"It's a promise, pretty. Dancing and games for all, you have my word." Bast raised his face for another long meeting of lips, nuzzling and warm. Then Bael was dressed and bending over Trick for a goodbye kiss.

Trick gave it easily, but kept it light; he was still too wrapped up in Bast to let Bael's taste take over his mouth.

Bael grinned as he backed away. "Don't let him forget, Trick-baby. A big party."

"Sounds like fun."

Trick watched Bael go, happy to see the grating close behind him and hear the elevator start its upward journey.

Bast curled back around him with a soft, happy hum. "Better?"

He nodded. "It's not that I don't like him, I just..." He shrugged. "It's not the same when it's not just the two of us."

"Yeah. Difference between playing and... not." Bast grinned at him, eyes twinkling.

"Yeah." He couldn't help but grinning back, though it soon faded.

"Would you... can you tell me about being a vampire? I mean. How'd it happen? How's it work? If you don't want to that's okay, I guess. I'm just curious, you know?"

"Slow down. I'll tell you whatever you want to know." Bast chuckled, wrapping the blankets over them both, the look on his face completely sated and relaxed. "One question at a time. What first -- how? When?"

"Yeah. Tell me about when it happened." He slid his hands against Bast's skin, loving the soft, silky feeling of it. Hard to believe this skin was 750 years old.

"It was really simple, believe it or not." Bast shrugged. "My family was running from the Plague and ran right into it. There we were, Mana, Pateras, all my brothers and sisters -- dying one by one. There were five of us left when Elizabeta, my nurse, came and infected us, made us brykolakas. Two of us survived."

"What happened to the other three? And brykolakas -- that's Greek for vampires?"

"Yeah, sounds cool, doesn't it?" Bast's smile dimmed. "It doesn't work like the movies, you know. It's a virus, close as they can tell. It mutates the bone marrow. To infect someone, you remove almost all their blood and then insert infected blood.

"Think about, these days, the right equipment? You can replace the blood and your chances of survival are good. But then?" Bast shook his head. "They died and for years I believed they were the blessed ones."

Trick made a soft noise, kind of a whimper, but not, and wrapped Bast up in his arms. "How long? he asked. "How long before you found happiness?"

"Happiness?" Bast's eyes flashed up to the painting, the darkness softening, easing into something he wasn't sure he understood. "That's a relative term. It took six years before Cecilia and I could travel. A decade more before I was strong enough to leave the caves alone. Forty beyond that before I moved on my own."

"Sixty years! That's like a lifetime. I can't imagine... I mean thirty seems ancient, let alone sixty."

He just held Bast for a while, trying to absorb it all, trying to make it feel real.

"How does it work? The being a vampire, I mean, not becoming one."

Bast shrugged. "No sun, food sits like a rock. My metabolism is non-existent. I'm not dead, but I'm not alive, not really. I... there are people like me who spend lifetimes explaining and researching. I just follow the rules -- no sun, eat blood at least once a moon cycle, stay in your own fucking territory."

"Your own territory? What's that mean?"

"This place is mine, not that there's another one of us here that I know of." Bast blushed. "We're territorial, in our feral stage, hungry, you know? There are some... odd complications about imprinting on a place, a person, and this asshole, knee-jerk *mine* shit happens. It's why I landed over here. Less competition means less growling feral shit." Bast rolled his eyes. "It's *so* hard on the skin and clothes."

He laughed like he knew Bast wanted him to and then he nuzzled close. "I guess that's all the questions I've got for now. Is there anything that I should know? Like vampire hunters coming after you and taking out anything in their way?"

"I'd be more terrified of Cecilia. She's a fucking bitch queen from hell."

He chuckled again. "Your sister, right? Oh, you're serious, aren't you?"

"Oh yeah. She's a vicious little whore." Bast's eyes flashed. "Just think about having to be a sixteen year old for seven hundreds years. Talk about *hormones*!"

Trick should his head. "I don't know -- I don't think I'd want to be a fifteen year old boy for seven hundred years either." He looked at Bast carefully, waiting for his reaction.

"The alternative at the time sort of sucked." Bast looked up and for a second, he looked positively ancient. Then that face was covered in a smile. "And not in the fun, spanky way either."

Trick smiled and Bast and held him close. "Are you happy now?"

"Yeah, Sweets. Yeah." Bast nipped at his throat. "I am now."

He gasped softly and pressed closer. "That's okay then."

Bast chuckled and nibbled again, this time a little harder. "Oh, yeah, sweet. Okay."

"You still hungry?" Trick asked, a shiver going through him.

"For you? Always, but I'd better not." No matter what he said, Bast pushed closer.

"Why not? I don't mind." He tiled his head back, body already thrumming with anticipation, his cock full, hard, pressing against Bast's thigh.

"Fuck, Sweets. Oh, fuck..." Bast pressed closer, groaning low. "You don't make it easy to be good."

"Depends on your definition of good, doesn't it?" His voice was husky and deep. It surprised him, how needy he was so soon after coming three times, but there was something about the feeling when Bast fed...

"Hungry... can't be hungry..." Bast's bites grew sharp, skin breaking and the hot tongue healing the wounds immediately. "Trick..."

He shuddered softly every time Bast bit him, hips beginning to hump frantically against Bast's leg.

"Bast. Please."

"Want to show you something. Trust me?"

"Okay, yeah."

Bast started licking down his belly, mouth heading directly for his aching cock. Those teeth looked sharp as they parted around his flesh. "Trust me."

Then Bast swallowed his cock down to the root.

Suddenly he didn't care about Bast's teeth, he didn't even think of them -- it was all about his cock and Bast's mouth and it was good. Bast sucked hard, pulling until Trick's hips were rocking into his mouth. Then he bit down and the world fucking dissolved.

He'd never screamed so hard in his life. Nothing had prepared him for this, absolutely nothing. He was coming, seed and blood pouring into Bast's mouth, down Bast's throat. *He* was pouring into Bast with every pulse of blood.

The world went red and then white and then, slowly, black.

When he came around, he was held tight in Bast's arms, covered in the blanket. He felt weak as a kitten, but unbelievably relaxed and good. He didn't think he could move, but that was okay, because he didn't want to.

"Wow." He said it softly, not trusting his voice.

"Good, then?" Bast's hands never left his skin. "Want a drink or is this okay?"

"Good? No, fuckin' great. An' this 's perfect. Don't wanna move, k?"

"I got nothing but time, Sweets." Bast hugged him tight.

"Oh, good."

He nuzzled, rubbing his cheek against Bast's. He couldn't keep his eyes open and he was so heavy. "Just gonna... nap."

Bast murmured something, but he was already too far into dreams to make it out.

Chapter Ten

Bast slithered into a pair of skin-tight leathers, buttoning them up halfway before shrugging into a loose maroon silk shirt that felt delicious on his skin. He gyrated gently to the music pouring through the flat as he tucked in and finished fastening, leaving the shirt halfway unbuttoned.

The furniture was pushed back, arranged into cozy little groups, the lighting dim, the music low and pulsating. The bar was stocked and kitchen was filled with little bits and starts of food.

Bast chuckled. Trick had been very insistent on munchies.

Speaking of munchies...

"Trick, Sweets? You dressed?"

"Define dressed."

Bast laughed, wandering toward the steamy bathroom. "Dressed. As in, with your clothes on and I can't beg a quick nibble from you, lovely."

There was a snort and then Trick appeared, framed by the doorway, black jeans on but not done up, beads of water still decorating the naked torso. "I'll never be *that* dressed, baby-boy."

"Oh..." Bast felt his body tighten, his gaze sharp and suddenly hungry, and he could smell Trick's musk beneath the soap and water. He reached out to stroke down the rippled belly and trail through damp blond curls, his cock painfully tight in the black leather.

Trick murmured and pushed toward him, groin first. Long fingers slid into his hair as Trick's lips ghosted over his. "Hungry, baby-boy?"

"Yes. Yes, Sweets." Bast let Trick see his hunger, let it shine free, knowing that his lover needed this, needed to know how much Bast longed and ached. He was shaking slightly, hunger exacerbated by the excitement of the party, the fun that was to come. "Please, love."

Trick's eyes met his, the blue as hungry as he felt, and the hands in his hair pushed, urging him down to his knees.

The leather creaked as it stretched, his body stretching and arching, the hunger making him supple. Trick's cock was hard, eager as it half-peeked from the open fly. Bast let his tongue trail along the exposed flesh. "Where, Sweets? Where do you want to feel me?"

One of Trick's hands slid from his hair and reached into his jeans, pulling out the hard flesh. "On my cock, baby-boy, want you to have it all."

"Trick..." That was all he got free before he bent to swallow Trick's flesh, sucking fiercely, letting Trick fuck his mouth. Then he grabbed Trick's hips, let his fangs nick the throbbing vein along the shaft.

Trick's scream of pleasure filled the air, echoing as Bast's mouth was flooded with seed and blood, salt and sugar blending together. The taste of Trick filled him and he cried out around his lover's cock, pulling in all Trick offered, shuddering as his hungers were sated.

He licked the wound gently, encouraging it to heal.

Trick's fingers were hard against his scalp and he could feel tremors pass through the hips he held, soft gasps replacing the lingering cry of pleasure that had rent the air.

He sucked for a moment longer, just enjoying the taste and feel of his lover in his mouth, on his tongue, *inside* him. Then he slid back and tucked the spent flesh back into Trick's jeans.

Arms looping around his neck, Trick leaned on him, mouth finding his blindly for a long kiss.

"Mmm... so good, Sweets. So fucking good." Bast was filled with passion and energy. "You okay? I didn't take too much?" He nuzzled Trick gently. "Wouldn't want you tired out for the fun."

Trick chuckled. "I thought that *was* the fun," he teased. "I'm fine. I'll just grab a protein shake and be good as new." The warm hands slid over his back. "Love the shirt, baby-boy. Blood and silk look good on you."

Bast grinned, preened for his lover.

"One day you'll let me dress you up. Although..." His eyes trailed over Trick's body. "Nobody does black like you, Sweets."

Trick grinned and preened right back, an impish mimic of his own moves. "What makes you think I'm going to wear a black shirt? I've got a couple of white tees, you know."

"You? In white?" Bast gave him a patently false shocked look, lifting his wrist to rest it against Trick's forehead. "Are you ill?"

Laughing, Trick nipped at his arm, teeth snapping at his skin.

Bast chuckled, throwing his arms around Trick's neck and pulling him down for a kiss. "Get dressed, lovely. Bael and his coterie will be here any minute."

Trick pressed a last kiss on him and then went back into the bathroom, returning seconds later, black t-shirt clinging to the lithe muscles. Touching Bast as he walked past him, Trick headed for the bar, quickly throwing together a protein drink.

Bast let his eyes trail over Trick, let himself drink in the long, lean lines of his lover. Fuck, but the boy was desire made flesh.

The rattle of the elevator warned them both that company was coming. "Ready to play, Sweets?"

Trick finished his drink and wiped away the moustache it left behind. "Greet your guests, baby-boy, I'm right behind you."

Bast lifted his head for a kiss, losing himself in Trick's mouth for a moment until Bael's soft drawl interrupted them. "Now, now, boys. It's not fair to get started without us."

Bast moved forward into Bael's open arms with a warm smile. "Oh, my pretty! It's been a while!"

Bael's hands settled on his waist, pulling him close and warm, wide lips closed over his in a deep kiss. "Too long. I almost wondered if I was going to need to start nagging you again."

"You know how quickly time flies when you're having fun." Bast smiled and leaned forward, whispering low. "He's good for me, pretty. Makes me fly."

Bael gave him a quick squeeze. "Well, that's good for you and bad for the rest of us. Though I suppose we'll forgive him if you have us in now and then for a bite." Bael winked outrageously and let him go.

Bast chuckled, moving to hug and kiss the little group of bright peacocks that were flowing in the door. It felt good, the pleasure these people felt at seeing him.

He looked back, Bael had his arm around Trick's waist, chattering happily, introducing Trick around. Bast grinned. Watching the peacocks flutter and play around Trick felt even better.

Trick was grinning and talking easily. Bast was probably the only one who noticed the soft tension that held his Sweets' spine straight, but he was already relaxing beneath the warm greetings.

"Apparently Trick's quite the dancer," Bael was saying, with another wink at Bast. "Come give us a taste of your moves."

Miranda slipped under Trick's free arm and joined Bael in enticing the boy further into the room, the raven-haired beauty's hips moving against his.

"Oh, Bast, we've missed you so, lover." Rose wrapped her arms around his shoulder, her bald head rasping against his cheek, whiskey and cigarette voice sliding down the front of his chest.

"I needed a bit of a break, mijita. Needed to escape." He turned and embraced her. "I'm back now and we'll play more. I haven't heard you sing in ages."

They were both enfolded in long broad arms and a deep, bass voice slid right down over Bast's spine. "So this is where you've taken to hiding?"

He was treated to a long, near bone-shattering hug by the man affectionately known as Bear to his friends. "Your boy looks pretty good out there."

Turning to look, he discovered Trick sandwiched between Bael and Miranda, the three moving like liquid sex to the throbbing beat rolling through the apartment.

"He moves like a fucking dream, Bear." Rose's hard, muscled body moved between them, her voice low and sultry. "Of course, our Bast, nobody fucks like him. He can make you scream."

Bast turned, lifting his head for the touch of Bear's lips, his hands sliding around Rose's waist and pulling her close. They moved slowly, sensuously, rocking and touching.

Trini and the twin blond brothers Zeph and Davo had made a beeline for the divan, dispensing with any of the evening's other activities for the pleasure of enjoying each other's bodies. Bast watched them for a while admiring the way the pale bodies of the boys moved in tandem as they rocked the black beauty between them.

"Bast, Bear, Rose -- come play with us, lovelies. Truth or Dare's not fun with just three." Bael and Trick were sitting on the bed, Miranda spread out before them, dark eyes challenging.

Rose chuckled, leaning forward to steal a long kiss. "Shall we play with them, lover? Make them scream."

Bast grinned and nodded. "I'm always up for a game, mijita. You know that."

"We'll see who screams first." Bael's eyes were full of mischief.

Trick grinned, a little bit of the tension back in his body; his Sweets didn't know what to expect. Bast moved to the bed, finding a place on Trick's lap and lifting his face for a kiss. "Truth or Dare's too fucking complicated, Bael. Let's play Spin the Bottle instead. Or we could play Spin the Dildo; that would please my sweet Rose."

Rose chuckled. "What, a girl doesn't get a kiss first?"

Bael pounced across the bed and kissed her soundly, sending the whole group into giggles.

Trick's arms came around his waist, chin resting on his shoulder as he watched the antics. Bast nuzzled back, filling himself with Trick's scent. He leaned back and murmured, "You okay, Sweets? You want to play?"

"'M fine." Trick's nose slid along his neck, tickling. "Just opening-night jitters."

Bael stood up. "I've got it! Babe, is your toy bag still in the same place?"

Bast grinned and nodded. "Yeah, pretty. It is."

He grinned as Bael disappeared into the bathroom. "We're in trouble, lovelies."

A bit of rustling and then a happy crow and Bael bounced out, heavy burlap bag in hand. "Okay, here's the game. You spin the bottle twice. The first person reaches into the bag and picks. The second person gets to play with you and the toy. Interested, babe?"

Bast chuckled. "You're a perv, Bael. No wonder we're friends."

"You'd best be getting out of the boy's lap now then or you'll cheat on who the bottle's pointed at when it heads your way."

Trick chuckled at Bear's words and gave Bast's neck a quick nip with his teeth before letting his arms unloop from around his waist and the group settled into a loose circle on the big bed.

Everyone looked expectantly at Bast.

Bast reached over and snatched Bear's beer from his hand, drinking it down quickly. Then he placed the bottle on the bed, comforter drawn tight by their weight. "Ready, lovelies?"

He spun the bottle, the mouth pointing to Bael. "Okay, pretty. Pick away."

Bael made a show of rummaging around the back, eyes going dramatically wide now and then, and in the end he pulled out a riding crop. "Oh, this is perfect, babe -- you've been such a bad boy, hiding from us."

"Oh, now... hiding is a strong word..." Bast grinned and reached for the bottle. "If I'm lucky, I'll get 'Randa. She's got a soft touch."

The bottle spun slowly and then pointed to Rose, whose dark eyes lit up. Bael handed her the crop and her muscles rippled, grin going feral. "Oh, lover. Come here, you wicked boy. Climb onto my lap and we'll make sure you don't hide from us again."

Bast chuckled and grinned, leaning forward to crawl across to her. "Now, mijita, I thought we were on the same side."

"Oh, we are -- remember that while I'm beating you and be thankful."

He was the center of their attention, five pairs of eyes on him, the hottest his Sweets'; he could smell his love's arousal tinged slightly with nerves.

"Thankful. Right." He crawled over Rose's lap, making sure his hand slid between Rose's thighs as he assumed the position. He grinned ferally over at Trick and then batted his eyelashes at Rose. "Be gentle with me. I'm a fragile flower."

Trick's laughter mingled with the others', the noise disguising the sound of the crop as it came down across his buttocks, Rose sparing him not at all.

Bast spread his thighs, settling onto his knees more comfortably, ass rocking up. The burn moved through him, bright and fucking sharp -- almost as sharp as knowing Trick was watching him. "Oh, Rose... you've been working out, mijita. Again. Let me feel it."

She brought down the crop again, and this time it zinged loudly through air in the silence that had fallen over them. And it fell again, Trick's sharp intake of breath drawing his eyes back to his Sweets as the crop fell.

Trick's eyes were dark, his breathing shallow, but for the odd gasp that sprang from him.

His ass was on fire, undulating over Rose's lap, entire body moving in response to the sweet blows and Trick's gaze.

Suddenly the blows stopped, Rose's hand sliding over his hot ass, pressing against the leather. She was panting lightly, and he could smell her arousal. "Fuck, lover. No one moves under the lash like you. Let me have my turn with the bottle now."

Bast nodded, kissing the short, callused fingers that wielded the crop before gingerly moving back to his place on the mattress.

Trick's hand slid silently over his thigh and squeezed gently, the question soft and unspoken, 'are you okay?'

He answered his lover with a hot, hungry kiss, drawing Trick's hand around to touch the heat pouring off his ass. Trick moaned into his mouth, squeezing his buttocks.

Rose cleared her throat loudly. "*My* turn, boys."

Bast leaned back with a feral grin, eyes feeling hot and swollen. "You don't want to cross her, Sweets. She's got a hell of a forearm."

They all laughed, watching Rose's bottle spin until it landed on Bael.

"Ah, good thing I didn't give the bag away." He grinned over at Rose. "I know *just* what you need, Rose love."

He dug for a moment, pulling out a pair of jeweled nipple clamps and dangling them from his fingers.

She licked her lips and ran her gaze around the circle. "Now who gets to put them on?" She spun the bottle again.

Bear grinned as the bottle stopped on him and held out his massive hands. "Off with the shirt, Rose baby. Let me decorate you."

She pushed her chest at him. "Oh, I think you should take it off, and don't worry about ripping it -- I'm sure the boys have something I could borrow to get home with in the morning."

Bast watched as Bear took her at her word and, hand on either side of the collar, the big man split the shirt in two, throwing the rag over his shoulder.

Trick's hand tightened on his buttocks, making it burn, almost distracting him as Bear tested the bite of the clamps, snapping them in the air.

"Oh, Rose baby, you're going to feel these and they're so sparkly." Bear bent forward to attach them onto Rose and Bast leaned into Trick, nuzzling close, grinning as Rose took a quick, sharp breath.

Bear lifted his head and murmured something, Rose nodding and wrapping her arms around his thick neck and offering a long, slow kiss as the other clamp was fastened. Bear pulled on them gently and then gasped himself as she bit down on his lip. "Cheeky."

She only grinned up at him and shook her chest, making the jewels dance on her nipples before handing the bottle over to him.

Bear chuckled and spun, the bottle pointing toward Bast, who laughed merrily. "Oh, Bear! What is in my little bag for you?"

Bael handed the bag over, Bast taking it and digging through until his fingers found a soft, fur-covered glove. He pulled it out, grinning widely. The last time he and Bear and Rose had played, they'd had the big man shuddering with pleasure, begging for release.

Bear blinking slowly and shivered, reaching down slowly to spin the bottle again. Miranda's red-tipped hands reached for the glove the moment the bottle stopped.

"Clothes off, Bear. You're all mine."

Bear undressed quickly, revealing surprisingly hairless skin beneath the dapper clothing. He was erect, penis as large as the rest of him, and Trick took a sharp breath and swallowed tightly.

"That's our 'Randa. All or nothing for our girl." Bast's voice was light and warm, slightly husky as Miranda began to stroke along Bear's skin.

Rose crawled next to Trick, eyes fastened on her lover. "He's beautiful, isn't he? Not sexy like you, but rough and so susceptible to pleasure."

"Pleasure makes people beautiful." Trick's voice was husky too. "Makes them glow."

"Yes. That's what this is about, yeah? Glowing together?" Bear was arching and moaning softly as Miranda played him, and finally Rose spoke up. "Enough, 'Randa. Let him come down, girl. We'll build him back up later."

Miranda nodded, bending to lick the sweat from the hollow of Bear's shoulder and reaching for the bottle.

The bottle spun and stopped at Trick. He grinned and reached into the bag, pulling out the first thing he touched. Miranda squealed with delight as his hand came out with a wide purple dildo.

She spun the bottle again, already shimmying out of her dress, leaving on her garter and stockings as the bottle came to a stop in front of Bael.

Bael grinned and held out his hand for the dildo, sliding his hand along the plastic.

Bast reached into the bag, digging until he found a little vial of oil that heated to the touch. At Miranda's arched eyebrows, he shrugged. "To ease its way, beauty, of course."

Then he tossed the oil to Bael.

She spread herself out in the middle of the bed, black laced legs spread, one foot resting against Trick's thigh, the other against Bast's. Trick traced the designs in the lace along her sole with one fingertip, making her wriggle.

Bast let one of his hands trail along Miranda's legs, his other hand sliding over Trick's belly, tracing along the jumping muscles.

Bael knelt beside her, bending low to take a long, deep kiss, sliding the dildo along her belly, leaving a slick trail.

Her leg muscles tensed and she pushed up, eagerly searching for the sensation she knew was coming. Her hand closed over Bael's wrist, pushing the dildo down to her opening.

Bast lifted her foot, watching Bael tease her. As the dildo pushed inside her, Bast bent his head and nipped at her ankle, grinning as she moaned.

Bael's dark eyes met his, his hand moving the dildo in slow, long strokes as Miranda arched. "Don't start biting, babe. This game'll get serious."

"We're not serious?" Bast grinned and nodded, placing Miranda's foot back onto his lap. She made a soft sound of disappointment and slid both her heels over, digging into his and Trick's groins, just hard enough to register her complaint.

Bael chuckled and pulled the dildo out. "This round's play only, pretty lady. You'll have to wait to come, just like the rest of us."

He took the bottle up and spun it between her legs with a sharp twist of his wrist. Rose crowed as the bottle pointed to her. She grabbed the bag from Bast, jeweled chain swinging and catching the light. Digging deeply, she came up cock ring with a pair of tiny nipple clamps attached with a long chain. "Oh, Bael. Won't these look lovely on you?"

Bael chuckled and spun again, the bottle pointing to Trick.

Rose handed the ring and clamps over. "Make him glow, Trick."

Bast watched Trick's face, running his hand along the boy's stomach again. A light flush rose to Trick's face, and Bast could smell the sweet blood as it rushed so close to the surface. The muscles in his stomach were jumping, but his hands were steady as held the toys while Bael regaled them all with a slow striptease.

Finally naked, he crawled back onto the bed, knees spread wide as he stopped in front of Trick. "Do I get a kiss first?"

Trick laughed and nodded, bending, but bypassing Bael's lips in favor of his nipple, kissing the dark flesh and worrying the nub to hardness between his teeth. Bael's moan was loud and his hands slid into Trick's hair, jerking slightly as the first clamp bit into his flesh.

Trick leaned back again, wide confident grin on his face now, eyes holding Bael's gaze as he tweaked the other nipple between his thumb and forefinger.

Bael's eyes dropped closed as the second clamp found its home.

Bast shuddered, his own nipples hard as he watched Trick move. That hint of predator, that confidence, was what had drawn Bast's eyes that first evening, made him proposition his Sweets.

It made him shiver with desire, watching Trick play.

Another kiss found its way onto the black flesh, this one at the tip of Bael's cock as Trick's fingers slid the cock ring down to the bottom of Bael's shaft.

Straightening again, Trick pulled Bael to hardness, the fingers of his other hand pulling randomly at the chain, tugging on both nipples and cock. As Bael's mouth opened on a moan, Trick leaned forward and kissed him, long and deep, making Bael shudder.

One last stroke of the black man's cock and Trick was pushing him gently back.

"Play only," Trick said softly, chuckling at Bael's groan.

His Sweets picked up the bottle, turning to give him a heated look before spinning.

The bottle pointed to Bast and he grinned, leaping for the bag. What to choose for his boy? What to make him hard and hungry?

His fingers roamed, finally landing on a little device, a series of vibrating fingerpads -- a nipple or cock or sensitive area caught between two or three of the fingers was devastating. Bast grinned and pulled it out, the needy moans of the others on the bed testifying to the wisdom of his choice.

They all leaned in as Trick spun the bottle once more, everyone but Bael sighing with disappointment as the bottle stopped in front of the black man.

Trick laughed. "That'll teach me to tease you."

"Oh, yeah. I'll make you ache to do it again." Bael stretched out his hand and Bast moved to strap the gadget on. "Lose the clothes, Trick. I'm going to make you feel so good."

Trick stood and pulled off his t-shirt and then pushed down his jeans. His body was flushed, excited, cock hard, nipples raised. He stood there, hands on his hips. "How do you want me?"

Bael's eyes flashed and he opened his lips to speak when Rose leaned forward, whispering into his ear. Bael nodded and looked at Bast. "Wriggle out of those tight pants, babe, and hold your boy still for me. We want to see how you fit together, let you feel his need."

Bast shuddered and nodded, sliding the leather pants off, the silk shirt off his shoulders. Then he knelt behind his Sweets, hard cock snug against the crack of Trick's ass, holding Trick's hands in his own. "Gonna feel so good, Sweets. So fucking hot."

Trick leaned back, lips open and searching for his, closing their mouths together with familiar hunger. Bast drank the pleasure from Trick's mouth, hips rubbing against him. Trick was relaxed and hot, mouth open and needy.

A low hum filled the air and then Trick jerked, the kiss ending with his cry. Bast looked down to see dark fingers holding a taut nipple, squeezing and pulling slowly.

Trick's hands squeezed his, the blond head flung back against his shoulder as his Sweets rode the sensations.

Bael played the same nipple until Trick was sobbing, hips pushing forward and dropping back rhythmically. Bast moved with each undulation, Trick's body hot and smooth and alive before him. He could feel the eyes on them, admiring the sensuality and sheer fucking beauty of his Sweets in pleasure.

Bael's fingers trailed down to Trick's abdomen, tracing the quivering muscles, giving Trick a moment to catch his breath.

The grip on Bast's hands had loosened somewhat when Bael began to play with Trick's other nipple and Bast heard his name called out, Trick's voice thick with pleasure, trembling with need.

"Oh, yeah, Sweets. Feels so good, doesn't it?" Bast began you run his lips over Trick's throat, feeling the life pulsing beneath the smooth skin. So close. So hungry. "You look so fucking beautiful, lover. Makes me hungry for you. Makes me want to drink you in."

"Yes." Trick's response was immediate and affirmative, as it always was since he'd accepted Bast's peculiarities.

"No, no, not yet boys." Murmurs of agreement joined Bael's denial and Trick whimpered.

"Bael! Pretty! I need..." Another pass of his lips, another press of Trick's body, another pulse of sheer, pure desire. Bast let his need show, eyes burning across at the group that watched them with such fascination. "I'm hungry, Bael."

"Just let me..." Bael's voice trailed off as his hand moved down again, sliding past Trick's belly and into the nest of curls and the prize they surrounded.

Trick's whole body arched as Bael's hand moved over his cock and then he slammed back hard against Bast. His eyes were closed tight, body shaking, straining.

"Sweets..." The word was snarled, animal held just within the grasp of his tattered humanity. Bast bit down, world going crimson as the hot, sweet splash of blood filled his mouth, moans and screams and sighs of various timbres just registering beneath the overwhelming beat of Trick's pulse within his head.

Trick's body shuddered and shook within his arms and then grew limp and heavy against him.

Bast licked and laved the sweet skin, lapping every trace of blood away, before easing Trick to the mattress. He bent to take a kiss, focus complete on his lover.

Trick's mouth opened to him immediately, one hand sliding up into his hair, cradling his scalp as Trick let him feed from the delicious mouth, taking passion and love from his Sweets. They kissed for long, breathless moments, bodies entwined, rocking together slowly, letting warm desire build between them again.

Other hands slowly introduced themselves into the embrace, stroking and petting, encouraging soft moans and arches. They were turned onto their sides and Bast felt a warm body press close behind him, Bear if the size of the cock nudging at his entrance was anything to go by. Someone else was pressed up against Trick's back and they were blanketed by skin as well, all them writhing and moaning together, pleasure shared, increased, pushing everything but itself away.

Bast floated, buoyed by the flavor of Trick in his mouth, the dazed pleasure in the face before him, the passion-drugged moans and sobs that filled his ears. A pale wrist appeared at his lips and he bit down, drawing the smoldering dark flavor of Rose inside him, sucking softly, eyes on Trick's face.

Passion and jealousy flared there and then, eyes fastened to his, Trick pushed his tongue between Bast's lips and Rose's wrist, slick against his incisors and stealing several drops of blood for himself.

Bast moaned, attention drawn by the addictive taste of Trick's mouth, of his tongue, of *him*. Together their tongues moved over Rose's wrist and then, as it fell away, their lips melded together.

Bear pushed into him, the large cock filling him and pressing him harder into Trick, even as Trick gasped into his mouth, shoved hard against him by Bael. The ladies' soft hands moved over them, murmuring encouragement as the four men moved together.

Trick's cock was hard against him as they writhed together. Someone's hand pulled his leg up over Trick and Bael, opening him further for Bear's deep thrusts. His fingers were moving over Trick's face, in Trick's hair, their lips refusing to part, tongues hungry as they feasted.

Hands, legs, cocks, bodies pressed together, wrapped in and against each other. It was becoming hard to tell where his pleasure ended and others' began.

Sharp fingernails found his nipples; someone's callused fingers circled his and Trick's cocks; warm, soft lips fastened onto the nape of his neck. He arched, nipping against Trick's lips. The bright tinge of blood hit his tongue and Bast came, body overwhelmed with sensation.

He felt well fed and invigorated, warmed by the bodies that pressed all around him. The air smelled of sex and blood and satisfaction.

He took another soft, lazy kiss from Trick, smiling at the low, sleepy, satiated murmur that he received in return. Bael's dark eyes gleamed at him, his friend lapping gently at the salt on Trick's skin.

"He's a sweet one, your boy."

Trick made a snort of protest and half-heartedly attempted to shrug Bael off, but soon gave that up for snuggling tightly against Bast. Bast drew Trick close, wrapping around the warm, relaxed body. His mouth closed over the join of shoulder and throat -- not biting down, just resting his teeth lightly enough for Trick to feel. Bael's eyes widened as Bast staked his claim.

Nothing was said, beyond Trick's soft sigh and utter relaxation into his arms. Nothing needed to be said at all.

***

He wasn't sure if it was the rattle of the elevator, the opening of the refrigerator, or the desperate need for a shower that woke him.

Bast opened his eyes in time to see Miranda and Trini disappear along with the twins as the elevator grate closed. Bael was leaning against the doorframe leading to the kitchen, glass of juice in his hand.

"They gone already?"

Bael nodded. "The girls had to work and the twins had another gig. You know how they are."

Bast grinned. "Fuck, I need a shower in the worst way." He extricated himself from the pile of Trick and Bear and Rose, managing not to wake any of them, and padded towards the bathroom.

Bael set his glass down on a counter and trailed after him. "You want company, lover?"

"Sure, pretty one. I'll scrub your back." He smiled and held out his hand to Bael, grasping his friend's fingers warmly.

He turned the water on, letting the room fill with steam, fogging the newly installed mirror, before stepping beneath the spray. Bast moaned softly as the water beat down on his muscles, relaxing and cleaning. "Man, showers are the world's greatest invention."

Warm, knowing hands joined his, slick with soap and gliding boldly. "You hungry, Bast? Need a little more sugar?"

When he didn't answer right away Bael slid a hand around his skull and pulled him down to the ebony neck. "The boy's not here to see, take what you want."

Bast lifted his head, frowning. "What the fuck are you talking about, Bael?"

Trick knew he needed more blood than one person could provide, knew that Bast needed to feed. Right now, Bast could still taste Trick on his tongue, was still full and fed on his Sweets. He didn't need and now, with Trick, if he didn't *need*, he wasn't interested in looking for other flavors.

"I'm talking about this little possession kick the two of you seem to be on -- the boy stopped you from feeding *and you let him.* And then that little show of ownership you laid on him." Bael shook his head. "You're both playing a dangerous game, my very old friend."

"You don't know what you're talking about, Bael. I'm more than old enough to know who I want, what I want. Christ! We all just finished fucking like bunnies! Those are not actions of possessive people." Bast looked at Bael, not quite sure he understood. "I don't own Trick, any more than he owns me, but I guarantee you, I'm not playing a game with him."

He turned his face up to the water, shaking his head. "I don't see your problem."

"When's the last time you fed from something that either wasn't Trick or came out of a bag?"

"It's been a while." Bast shrugged. He couldn't remember, although he imagined it was during the dark hunger when he was hiding, when Bael came every few weeks to keep him alive and sane, or maybe when they'd played with Bael the last time he'd visited.

"This isn't like you, lover. You're the ultimate free soul. You party, you have a good time, you feed off of whoever's available. You certainly don't turn down an offer to feed." Bael shook his head. "I've known you for a long time and you've never been exclusive before."

Bast sighed, turned into the spray. Not like him? Bael had played with him for what? Ten years? Fifteen? No one knew him -- not his friends, not his family, not even Trick. No one since... "Bael, drop it."

"You tell me one thing and I will -- if that kid came in here right now and offered you what I did, would you turn him down like you did me?"

"Yes, Bael, I would." Bast turned, eyes serious. "Don't do this to us, pretty. Don't get all pissy. I never promised you anything but fun and pleasure, and I gave you what I said I would."

He moved into Bael's arms, giving his friend a warm hug. "I'm not out of circulation, pretty. We'll play until you're old and grey and only interested in using my face to get you pretty girls."

"I'm more worried you're going to take off again if something spooks Trick. I don't have to have you if you're happy as you are, Bast. I just don't want to lose you because you have too many eggs all in the same basket. I won't pretend I know what's going on between you and him, but I saw what you were like the last time he left."

Bast nuzzled softly against the warm, dark skin, hiding the tears that threatened. "You're so good to me, Bael. No one ever took care of me like you do."

Bast kissed Bael's shoulder, the smooth, easy, familiar flavor of his skin comfortable on his tongue. "I would be dead if it weren't for you, pretty, or gone animal on the streets. I won't desert you."

"You're too lovely a creature to let go feral and be killed." Bael's lips fell silent beneath the weight of his own, the familiar hand running down along his spine to curve over his ass, pulling them together.

Bast smiled, body responding to the warmth and friendship Bael offered, had always offered. Bael tasted of safety and peace and trust, the passion he engendered slow and easy, sweet and still.

They made long slow love, finishing each other off with their hands, seed spilling into the shower's spray and washing away.

Bast purred softly, body relaxed and sated, the hot water finally beginning to cool. "Come on, pretty. Let's find our place in the pile."

Bael chuckled. "Your place is in the center, Bast. As it should be."

He grinned and took another kiss. "My pretty lover, what would I do without you to stroke my... ego?"

Bael's rich chuckle floated warmly over him.

It faded slowly away, Bael staring at his own image in the mirror. "I never thought I'd see one of these in here."

"Trick likes it. I don't even notice it." Bast grinned and pressed up against Bael's back, invisible in the glass. He tweaked a dark nipple, chuckling as the flesh seemed to move on its own in the mirror. "Almost like being invisible, huh?"

Bael shook his head, but didn't say anything. He turned from the mirror and gave Bast a quick kiss before taking his hand and leading him back to the bed. "Come on, it's early yet -- I think we should come up with some way to torture the three on that bed who flaked out on us. Something devious and wickedly sexy."

"Mm...devious sounds promising. You have any brilliant ideas or shall we just get out the whips and chains?" Bast grinned as his eyes wandered over the tangle of limbs. Rose had shifted until her cheek was nestled against the small of Trick's back, Bear large enough to appear to circle them both.

"I was thinking of tying them down and waking them up in the old fashioned way," Bael replied with a malicious wink.

"Ah, yes. Red-hot pokers and the rack!" Bast grinned over and he and Bael burst out laughing.

"You know, if you're going to sneak up and ravish us, you should try being quiet, boys." Rose muttered, rubbing her cheek against Trick's back.

Trick came awake at that, sitting up and blinking, startled. Seeing Bast, he relaxed, stretching his arms up over his head. "Speaking of ravish -- I'm starving. Anyone else want something?"

"That's my Sweets, always hungry." Bast crawled onto the bed, Trick giving him a long, slow kiss. "There's plenty of food, lovelies. Help yourselves."

Bear's head lifted up and he grinned. "Food? You have food, Bast? Since when?"

Bast chuckled. "I'm always being questioned. Go. Eat."

He curled up upon the bed, steadfastly ignoring Bael's eyes.

Trick leaned down for another kiss, tongue licking across his lips and then following the line of his jaw back to his ear. "You want a snack first, baby-boy?"

A slow shiver and he shook his head, forcing his hunger back. "No, Sweets. Not so soon. We wouldn't want you pale and shaky, lover."

He could feel the accusatory look coming from his friend; Bast just closed his eyes.

"Oh." Disappointment and hurt filled the sound and then he felt Trick shrug, knew his Sweets was putting on his game-face. "Okay. But I'm still starving."

The bed shifted as Trick got up and Bast could hear the bare feet pad toward the bar.

Bast buried his face in the pillows, pushing close to Rose's warmth, mind whirling, body beginning to rumble and ache. He hadn't fed from Trick every day since they'd come back from uptown. Surely he hadn't. He wouldn't.

He heard Trick pour out and toss back a bourbon, senses hyperaware of his Sweets' movements.

He opened his eyes, watching Trick move. Bast could taste the sweet-salt of Trick's skin, the rich, dark flavors of Trick's seed, Trick's blood. He could feel the hunger within him, stronger than it should be, more insistent. When Trick's gaze met his, he moaned softly, his breath brushing over Rose's calf.

Trick's eyes reflected his own hunger back at him, the longing in them a physical touch.

He was standing, moving towards his lover before he quite knew what he was doing, hands reaching up to brush the thick hair away from Trick's face, body pressing close. "That booze isn't going to ease your hunger, Sweets."

Trick's arms wrapped around him, mouth descending to take his, to feed from him with such hunger, hunger that no drink or food would satisfy. Bast sighed into Trick's mouth, his own need easing as his comfort grew. He was used to this now, used to the smell and taste and feel of Trick in him, on him, surrounding him.

He slid his arms around Trick's neck, lips parting wider. And Trick thought *he* was addictive.

"Oh, fuck, they look good together." Rose's voice, sleepy and slurred, slid over his consciousness.

Trick began to rock him against the bar, hard thrusts that were echoed by the nips of teeth that covered his face. He lifted his knee, curling his leg around Trick's hip and pulling him closer. Hanging on, Bast rode the waves of need and pleasure and desire, eyes still fastened onto his lover's.

Trick's eyes widened as he came, body still moving against Bast, the way suddenly slick and easy.

"Oh, Sweets. So good." He buried his face in Trick's neck, just licking the skin, letting the sweet flavor fill him. Someone cleared their throat, and he suddenly remembered they weren't alone. He smiled, warmth filling him. It felt good, to lose himself in his lover's arms.

Trick's hands slid over his skin in a possessive caress and another kiss was dropped onto the top of his head. Snagging a power bar, Trick let him go and wandered back toward the bed, seeming unconcerned with his nudity or the seed that stuck to his skin.

Bast poured himself two fingers of bourbon, belting it down before wandering back to the bathroom and jumping back in the shower, the liquor burning his throat, eyes burning in his head, lukewarm water sliding over his skin.

He reached out and turned off the light, just letting himself feel the water.

He wasn't sure how long he'd been standing there when Trick came up behind him, cradling his body against warm flesh. His Sweets' mouth moved gently along his shoulder, licking at water and skin.

Bast sighed, relaxing back against him, soaking up the welcome heat.

Trick's hands moved over him, gentle and loving. "I sent them away."

"Thank you." Bast relaxed into Trick's hands. "Oh, Sweets, you feel good."

He didn't know what to say, what to think.

So he simply felt.

For a long time Trick simply touched him, body warm and soft and hard behind him. Then Trick's wrist pressed against his lips, his Sweets' voice husky and rough in his ears. "Take what you need, baby-boy."

He fastened his mouth on Trick's wrist, nibbling gently on the tender skin before sliding one fang in. It pierced the vein easily, blood welling up into his lips. He sobbed as he drank, feeding his body and soul with his lover.

Trick moaned and shuddered against him, arm tight around his waist, holding them together.

He suckled at the skin even after he sealed the wound, whispering his love and need against the web of veins.

It was Trick who leaned past him and turned off the water, Trick who wrapped them both in towels and got them to the bed; his lover's body curled around him warm and solid and real.

Bast sighed, nuzzling close, anchoring himself in Trick's hands, in the beat of Trick's heart. He rested in Trick's embrace, let his concerns shatter in the back of his mind.

"Love you, Sweets." The whisper was soft enough that Trick could pretend he hadn't heard it, but Bast would know it was said.

A half sigh, half sob sound came from Trick and his Sweets' arms tightened around him, pulling him closer.

Bast rested his head, closed his eyes and let Trick's heartbeat soothe him into a sleep, whispering soft secrets they both could hear.

CHAPTER ELEVEN

Trick sighed with relief as he closed the elevator behind them. They were alone at last.

They'd been dancing, Rose, Bear, Bael playing under the lights with them. Bael had been pushing to come home with them, said it was too long since he had a "Bastgasm."

Trick had pleaded a headache, insisted for tonight he just wanted to go to bed and have Bast curl around him, warm and quiet. For a moment, he thought Bael was going to fight him on it, but the black man had nodded and let them go.

He sighed again, wanting to lock the door with him and Bast inside and the world outside and never unlock it again.

Bast was frowning, hands roaming up and down his arms. "Sweets? You need something? Aspirin? Food?"

Leaning back against the grating, he looped his arms around Bast's waist and pulled him close. "Just you."

"Oh, that I can do." True to his word, Bast snuggled, arms wrapping around his neck, lips nuzzling at his throat.

"Mm..." He pulled Bast close and half picked him up off the ground, walking them together the bed.

No one could snuggle quite like Bast, hands sliding under clothes and over skin, lips and cheeks pressing and caressing. He worked his own hands into Bast's clothing, laughing as his attempt to make his lover naked was impeded by the tightness of the cat suit Bast wore. The man sure looked good in them, but they were hell to take off.

Bast chuckled into his mouth, wriggling against him as they worked to get the emerald velvet off without tearing it.

By the time he and Bast were naked, Bast's eyes were glittering and happy and Trick was warm, happy, and eager for the feeling of Bast in his arms.

"Fuck, I love this. I mean -- I like partying and all, but stuff like this -- you and me and laughing and naked and... well it's good."

Bast nodded, grabbing an edge of the coverlet and wrapping them both up in it so they were cocooned in silky warmth. "This is real. We're real."

"Yeah..." He cupped Bast's head and pushed it toward his neck. "You hungry, baby-boy?"

"For you? Always, Sweets." Bast wrapped around him, holding him close, lips open and pulling against his skin.

"Then feed, baby-boy, please." He arched his neck, giving Bast as much room to work with as possible. He could feel Bast's need in every beat of his own heart; it became his own. "Please."

"Yes, Sweets." Bast's tongue was hot on his neck and he didn't even feel the bite this time. The pleasure and warmth and sensation of being held and needed simply deepened and grew -- the world dissolving in a slow, breathless rush.

He came, he always did when Bast fed, but that was only a physical manifestation of the way it felt, the way the pleasure filled him as his blood filled Bast. It was like they were joined, like they only had one heart and his blood filled them both.

Trick floated back into his body, wrapped close in Bast's arms, dark eyes watching him. "Hey, Sweets. Welcome back."

"Hey." He felt weak but good. Amazing. He raised his face for a kiss.

Bast's lips were hot, alive, full, moving over his own. He moaned softly, tasting himself there, more than just a flavor, something deeper, something that went with the feeding. The kisses came, one after another, some deep, some shallow, until he was dizzy and breathless and utterly relaxed.

"This is mine," he murmured softly, barely aware he'd spoken the words aloud.

"Trick?" Bast's head tilted, eyes sharp.

His cheeks grew hot and he looked down, biting his lip. "I don't... fuck it, Bast -- it hurts when you feed from someone else. And I don't just mean emotionally, I mean it hurts underneath my skin."

"Hurts? Really hurts?" Bast frowned, stroking Trick's face. "What kind of hurt?"

He shrugged, feeling silly, but blundering on. "Like a burning itch, I guess. Like I know that it's me you're supposed to be feeding from, not Rose or Bael or *anyone* but me."

Bast stared at him, eyes glowing suddenly as if he were hungry, starving, face feral.

"I'm sorry," he said softly. "Are you gonna get mad if I ask you to... to only feed from me or the bagged blood?"

Bast reached for Trick's hand, drawing it down to his throbbing cock, a soft growl filling the air. "No, not mad. Not mad, Sweets."

"Oh..." He wrapped his hand around Bast's cock and started to pull. "All right, then. I want you to only feed from me."

"Yes, Chosen." Bast leaned forward, taking his lips in a hot kiss, cock pistoning in his hand.

Chosen. The word sent a shiver down his spine.

Made him hot.

He wrapped his free hand around Bast's back and pushed his hips up against Bast, one hand still wrapped tight around his lover's cock.

Bast groaned, eyes bright, focused on him, growls pouring into his lips.

"Take it." he spoke fiercely, his words almost a growl to match Bast's. "Seal the bargain with my blood."

"Yes, Trick. Chosen." Bast looked up at him, eyes wild. "Never letting you go again. Need you. You know that."

He nodded and arched his head back, exposing his neck once more to the vampire. "I know it. Seal the vow in blood, baby-boy. Feed."

Bast struck quickly, biting deep, pleasure blazing across his nerves.

He screamed, the joining almost too much. Almost. The world went pink and then red and then became nothing more than a single, slow heartbeat. The entire time, Bast was there, anchoring him into his body, bringing him back into the world of colors.

He looked up into Bast's eyes, a wide smile slowly pulling his lips wide. "Wow."

"Yes." Bast kissed the corner of his mouth, eyes bright. "Yes, Sweets."

"So you aren't going to bite anyone else now, right?"

"No one else." Bast kissed him again. "This is yours."

His. He'd never had anything that was his before. Oh, Bast had given him the warehouse, but that wasn't the same thing, not at all. This... feeding was something necessary to him and it was his.

"Thank you."

He got a smile in response and those dark eyes glittered. Then, Bast settled against him, humming softly, holding him tight, as if he were too precious to risk losing.

It felt good. It felt great.

He nuzzled close and closed his eyes, not going to sleep, just enjoying the sensation of being held, being wanted, needed.

At some point, he thought he heard Bast's whisper, "My Chosen. I've waited so long." But then the humming started up again and he might have been dozing because he was so warm and so relaxed and just right.

Eventually he fell asleep, the sound of Bast's happiness following him into his dreams.

CHAPTER TWELVE

"Thank you." Trick smiled at the waitress as she put his steak in front of him and then grinned as she turned to Bast.

"Are you sure you don't want anything to eat, honey?"

"No. I'm dieting, thanks." Bast grinned at Trick and then up at the waitress. "The coffee's fine."

"Suit yourself. Either of you boys need anything else, you just holler now, okay?" She left without waiting for a response, shoes dragging ever so slightly across the linoleum.

Dino's Diner wasn't a classy joint, it wasn't even much of a diner, but the food was good, and at this time of night it was deserted and once she'd served you, Evelyn pretty much ignored you unless you really did holler.

Which was perfect for what Trick had in mind.

He cut into his steak, grin widening as the blood seeped from the rare meat. He put the first piece in his mouth, closing his eyes and smiling with satisfaction as he began to chew. A second piece and then a third quickly followed, satisfying the hard edge of his hunger.

The fourth piece dripped blood on his chin.

Bast's eyes were hot, fierce on his face. "Uh, Trick, Sweets, you've got some..." The hand that held out the napkin hardly trembled at all.

Trick feigned surprise and wiped at his chin with his fingers, bringing them to his mouth to suck off the juices. He moaned softly at the taste.

He felt Bast shudder, saw the slender hands tighten on the edge of the table. "Is it good?"

"Oh, yeah." He shifted, adjusting his sprawl slightly so that one of his knees pressed against Bast's. He cut himself another piece of meat and slowly raised it to his mouth, letting the blood drip onto his hand and out of the corner of his mouth. His tongue snaked out to lick at the sides of his mouth.

"Sweets..." Bast shifted in his seat, a low growl rumbling from his chest. "You're doing that on purpose."

"Enjoying my food? Damn right I'm doing it on purpose. I'm starving." He grinned. "You're looking a little peaked yourself. You want me to 'holler' for Evelyn?"

"Oh, yeah. Evelyn, darling? Can I nibble a bit on that sagging, nicotine-stained turkey wattle you call a neck?" Bast rolled his eyes. "You can only make that steak last so long, lover."

Trick nodded. "Gonna have a piece of pecan pie when I'm done. Unless you like the cheesecake better." He stopped his fork midway to his open mouth, staring into space a moment. "I know you can tell the difference in my blood -- so I'll let you choose." He popped the steak into his mouth, licking at the juices that again escaped passed his lips.

"Get the pecan." Bast reached out, stopping himself before he reached Trick's lips. He pouted slightly, eyes fastened on Trick's lips. "I want to do that."

"You can have pie if you want, baby-boy, nobody's stopping you," he said, deliberately misunderstanding.

The next piece of steak he picked up wasn't quite on his fork right and it fell back on his plate, sending the pool of warm blood it landed in spraying. Shaking his head, he used his index finger to collect the red liquid from the edges of his plate. Pulling his finger into his mouth, he sucked off the juices and then went back for more until the edges of the plate were their usual dull off-white.

"Don't want the pie..." Trick saw Bast's eyes flash, saw his lover fight down the natural reaction to the sight and smell of blood so close.

He quickly cut the rest of his steak up into strips and then began to eat them with his fingers. He held the strips above his mouth the way the Greek gods were fed grapes in the paintings at the museum, letting the blood drip into his mouth before slowly lowering the meat.

He cleaned his fingers between each piece, sucking and licking at them, murmuring and moaning as he did so.

With each bite, Bast's tension heightened. The distracted chatter had ceased. The knee resting against him shivered constantly. A low, almost-inaudible growling slid across the table.

When Trick met Bast's eyes they were glowing softly, a golden-green that ached with hunger. He felt that ache in his own body, in the pulse of his blood through his veins, thick, life-giving liquid that surged with each beat of his heart.

Glancing up at the front of the diner confirmed that Evelyn wasn't there; she was probably on her cigarette break. He hoped she smoked several. He pulled his lower lip into his mouth and bit down on it until the skin broke. He flicked his tongue out over his lips, letting the blood paint them like lipstick as he nonchalantly reached for the last piece of meat.

A whimper sounded, Bast keening softly, nostrils flaring as if scenting out the fresh blood within his reach. "Please."

Trick leaned over the table and grabbed the back of Bast's head, pulling him close. Using the tip of his tongue he gathered blood from the cut in his own lip and then painted Bast's lips with it. "Anything, baby-boy."

Bast snarled, tongue swiping out to taste before sliding in his mouth, licking at the cut on his lip.

The kiss lasted for a long moment, Bast's tongue searching his mouth determinedly, and then Bast sat back, panting softly. "Finish your supper, Sweets, and get the pie to go."

Trick ate the last piece of meat, reluctantly losing the taste of blood and Bast in his mouth. He took the roll and sopped up the blood, sucking it noisily from the doughy bun. The milk only took a moment to drink and then he got up and cut himself a piece of pie, leaning over the counter to snag a styrofoam container; Evelyn still wasn't back from her break.

He tossed two twenties on the table and held out his hand to Bast. "Ready when you are."

"I'm ready. Take me home, Sweets." Bast took Trick's hand, standing up and pressing close to whisper in his ear. "Wanna take you home, make you scream, fuck you long and slow and then bite you when you come. I'm *hungry*, Trick." The last words were growled, feral and wild.

He shuddered, cock suddenly painfully hard in his tight jeans. "Then we'd better feed you, baby-boy."

Bast's eyes flared again and his lover melted against him. He could feel the press of Bast's cock, the sharp touch of teeth as Bast nuzzled his throat. "Yes, now. Need to taste you."

A door beyond the counter banged and Evelyn's shuffling gait followed.

Trick planted a rough kiss on Bast's lips and then grinned, arousal singing through him, making him feel as bright as Bast's eyes. "Race you home."

Those bright eyes met his, predatory in their focus. "Yes. First one home gets to bind the other and play with the toy bag."

Before he could answer, Bast was gone.

He was out the door in a flash, but couldn't see Bast anywhere. Shrugging, he took off down the street at a run, heading for the alley that backed onto the warehouses. He was panting, gasping for breath as he let himself into their building, but still, when he threw open the grating he found a note taped to the back of the elevator. "Too slow, Sweets."

Grinning, he swiped his card and hit the button. He bounced on his heels, excitement running up and down his spine like bolts of electricity.

The apartment was dark when the elevator settled and he pulled the grating up. He stepped into the room, blinking to adjust his eyes to the darkness. Slender cool fingers slid down his arms, holding him in a surprisingly strong grip.

"Welcome to my parlor." Sensual, seductive -- Bast's voice was smoother than high-dollar whisky, sliding down his throat.

Trick bit back his moan but couldn't stop the sweet shudder that shook him and his voice was low when he spoke. "Do you think your web can hold me?"

"Oh, yes, sweet thing." A wet heat slid over his ear. "Do you know how long I've dreamed about you, bound and hard, bent for me over the red divan?"

Another shudder went through him and he hissed. "Since the day you met me, baby-boy."

"Yes." One hand tangled in the neckline of his shirt, tearing it clean down the front, and suddenly Bast was standing before him, mouth pressed against his chest. "Yes."

He tangled his hands in Bast's hair, tilting his lover's face up and melding their mouths together; if Bast wanted him bound, he'd have to work for it. It would be more fun for both of them that way.

In the dark, the odd whimpers and murmurs Bast made seemed more varied, louder, another vestige of humanity stripped away, leaving a being of sheer sensation. Bast fed him tiny, hungry sounds, pressing cool, naked skin fully against him.

He shrugged out of the remnants of his t-shirt and began to work on his jeans, mouth working hungrily against Bast's. Bast's hands helped him with the button fly, lips and tongue never still. Between them, they freed Trick's cock, Bast's hands moving to slide the denim over his hips.

When Trick tried to push the material out of the way, he found himself stopped short, his wrists encased in warm, supple, butter-soft leather cuffs.

"Oh... not bad." He tested the cuffs, finding them comfortable, but firm. "Okay, you've got my hands. Now what?"

"Now this." Bast's teeth fastened over his nipple, biting down sharply and then pulling fiercely, sparkling tingles pouring over his skin.

Gasping, his arms rose automatically to cup Bast's head; it made the sensations stronger, not being able to control them.

"So sweet, my Trick." Bast continued leaving biting, sucking kisses down his stomach and against his groin. The jeans were pulled away, leaving him naked, Bast's lips hot on his inner thigh.

He spread his legs as best he could, bound hands against Bast's head for balance. The air was cool against the places Bast had kissed him and against his cock. He was tight with anticipation, almost trembling as he waited for Bast's bite.

Bast nuzzled and licked, cheek smooth against Trick's body. Deep, sucking, open-mouthed kisses were pressed randomly -- hot touches that let Trick feel the weight of Bast's teeth but that never penetrated, never gave them both what they wanted.

"Bast..." His own voice was unrecognizable, hoarse with deep-seated need.

"Yeah, Sweets?" The answer echoed hunger. Bast's hands joined the action, sliding up between his legs to caress his balls and behind.

He whimpered. "Oh, baby-boy, I need you. Need you so bad."

"Mm... I'm right here, lover. Oh, fuck, I can smell you." Bast's fingers disappeared, returning slick and cool against his entrance, pushing inside him, even as Bast's mouth slid over the tip of his cock.

Broken sounds came out of his mouth as he trembled between the two sensations; caught between the need to push forward and rock back, he just stood there, letting Bast suck him, fuck him. He wasn't even sure why he was still standing, his legs were trembling so hard.

Bast kept him trapped, kept him caught between the long fingers and those hungry lips, kept him impossibly balanced between pleasure and frustrated need.

He couldn't move, couldn't take what he needed and his voice had disappeared, been replaced by something broken that couldn't make the words come, could only moan and whimper and make these noises like he'd never heard before. His entire world became those lips and fingers, everything else fading away; there was no floor, no air, no sounds or sights or feelings except for those Bast gave him.

He was sucked into a world where he was only cock and ass.

Then a bright spot of sensation tilted his orbit and the universe exploded, every nerve in his body screaming in a supernova of pleasure as the hungry lips fed, long fingers pushed and stretched.

He dissolved into liquid, sliding through Bast's lips, down Bast's throat, deep into the quiet, aged, still dark that crouched inside Bast -- feeding and fed as he quickened that slow-beating heart.

Time stopped as their hearts beat together, as they became one, his blood pumping through both of them, animating them.

He cried out as Bast's lips let him go, ripping them apart.

Bast caught him as he fell, cradling him close, lips warm and full and wet as they moved over his face. Soft whispers of nonsense words that felt like spring rain fell against his ears and skin.

With lips and hands and body, Bast soothed the ache of separation, bringing Trick back, settling him back inside his own body, inside the regular rhythm of his own heart.

He pushed his head against Bast's neck, letting the thick, slow pulse beat against his cheek.

The restraints were brushed away, removed with the same unthinking ease they were attached. Bast's fingers twined with his, holding on, the cool, thin palm pressing close to his own warm, square hand.

The connections were a pale echo of what they'd just experienced, but they soothed the empty places inside him.

"I can feel you, feel your passion and your fire inside my veins." The words floated over him, full of awe and love and wonder.

"Oh..." Bast's words spoke to something deep inside him, something that had been growing with each bite, with every moment he spent in the vampire's presence.

Today Trick gave it voice. "I love you."

Bast's fingers trembled, tightened slightly and then relaxed. "I love you," Bast said.

A sigh shuddered through him and he relaxed further against Bast, feeling heavy and sated, the aftermath of Bast feeding always a peaceful glow.

"I think, the next time you decide you want a steak, you should probably cook it here," Bast mused gently, voice tinged with easy laughter and incredible warmth. "You almost got attacked at the diner, Sweets."

"I must have been doing something wrong then -- I wasn't going for almost."

Bast gave a surprised, delighted laugh. "Oh, Sweets! You'll be the death of me! No pun intended, of course."

He chuckled and nuzzled Bast's neck, licking salt from the cool skin. "Not the death of you, the life of you." He mouthed the words silently against Bast's skin, barely giving them breath.

"Oh." Bast leaned back, looking into Trick's eyes with a stunned, sweet shock that melted into something indescribable and joyful. "Yes."

"Yes." Bast leaned forward and kissed him, eyes fastened onto his face as if he might disappear, dissolve into dust.

The kiss was deep and tender and he felt tears prickle at his eyes; there'd never been a lot of tenderness in his life. He blinked them away angrily, not wanting to miss a moment gazing into the dark eyes.

A cool hand cupped his cheek, stroking over his skin. Bast's eyes smiled at him, warm and welcoming and close, passion present but banked.

Trick realized he was happy, not just sated from sex and dazed by passion, but simply happy. He couldn't ever remember feeling this way before.

"I love you, Trick." Another soft kiss brushed against his lips, those dark eyes not flinching away, honest and simple and bare.

He smiled, the emotions sliding through him like really good scotch. "I love you, too."

It wasn't so scary to say it this time, in fact it felt pretty good to say it, to watch as the same warmth he felt inside him bloomed across Bast's face.

Bast nibbled on his lips, suckling and nipping lightly, hands beginning to move over his skin with purpose. "Come to bed?"

He laughed, body responding to the touches despite his languor. "Race you."

***

The music was blaring, bodies pressed close all around, jostling and bumping. Bast had lost Trick three songs ago, getting pushed closer and closer to the stage, unseen, disembodied hands sliding over him, teasing and touching.

Rose was singing, screaming out dark, growly words weighted down with a heavy bass line and a pounding percussion. Her bald head gleamed in the stage lights, eyes dark and lost in the music.

Bast grinned up at her, then turned and craned his neck, looking for his lover. He scanned the dance floor first and then the bar, but couldn't find Trick. The lighting changed modes, bright flashes of color strobing, making it impossible to make out more than hands and lips and cheeks, everything disparate, shattered.

He was never going to find Trick in this.

Just then a hand slid over his shoulder and into his open shirt, warm and sure against his skin, all the way to the top of his stomach, while a second hand curled around his hip, sliding across his groin to cup his cock.

He knew that scent, knew those hands in his bones. No one made him hungry like Trick. Bast wriggled his hips, hiding his grin. "Mm... should I scream that I'm being molested?"

"Oh, you know I like it when you scream." Trick's voice was like whiskey and cigarettes in his ear, breath warm against his skin.

"Do you?" He pushed back against Trick's body, letting his head fall back on the warm shoulder. "You going to make me scream, Sweets?"

"I think you know the answer to that, baby-boy." Trick was moving to the music, hips swaying sensuously with the bass. "The real questions are how loud, how long, when and where."

"Mm...yes." His arms lifted, curling around Trick's neck, stretching his body beneath Trick's hands. Trick's jaw was close enough to bite, and he licked along the bone, gathering salt and sweat and sex on his tongue.

Trick's hands slid over his body, hips moving against him, making love to him right there on the dance floor, their clothes the only thing keeping them from being arrested.

He let his legs part, rocking between Trick's thighs and hand. He could feel the eyes on them, burning and hungry. "I thought you didn't like fucking in public, lover."

"I don't." Trick began to suck on his neck, teeth and tongue biting and soothing. "But we're here, and I need you."

"Oh." Bast shuddered, tilting his head, offering more skin to Trick's mouth in a motion very similar to the one that had led to the last time he'd fed from his lover.

The thought of feeding made him ache. It had been over two weeks -- Trick needed to heal, to build his strength. Bast needed to prove he could control his need. They'd agreed to a month without feeding. They'd spent a lot of time out in public, avoiding temptation.

This was *not* avoiding temptation.

Trick shuddered, a sound like a broken sob coming from him. His teeth bit hard against Bast's skin and then suddenly, shockingly, his lover's warmth disappeared. "I can't..."

Bast spun, breath coming rough and quick. "Sweets? What's the matter?"

"I love you." Trick's mouth descended over his, hard and deep and quick, and then Trick turned, pushing his way through the crowd.

Frowning, an ache deep in his belly, Bast followed, refusing to let the crowd stop him, snarling low at the few children daring to separate him from his Trick.

The night air was cool, winds blowing steadily and he had to hurry to catch up with Trick's longer legs. "Trick? Sweets? Please, lover, talk to me. What did I do?"

Trick laughed, the sound bitter and not in the least humorous. He didn't stop walking. "It's not you, baby-boy. It's me."

"What? Trick?" Bast reached out, touched his arm. "Talk to me. Take me home, let me buy you coffee, hell, I'm easy, love. Just *talk* to me."

Head shaking, Trick stopped. "I can't be with you, Bast. If I spend another moment with you I am going to beg for you to feed. On-my-knees-crying-and-weeping-beg, Bast. Fuck, I need it. I need you so bad, baby-boy."

Arousal and hunger and sheer need slammed into him, slapping away the veneer of humanity he held up, leaving someone more feral than civilized.

"Trick." The word was laced with desperation. "Oh, fuck, Sweets."

"Shit. Oh, fucking shit, Bast."

Trick's hands were shaking as they wrapped in his hair and pulled his face into the warm neck. "Please, baby-boy, please. Please." Trick's voice was thick with tears and desperation.

Bast looked around, a low growl sounding louder than the wind. He pushed them back into an alley, into the shadows, pressing Trick against the rough brick. One hand pushed Trick's head back, rough and uncivilized as hunger overran control. "Need you."

Then he bit down, screaming as Trick poured into his mouth.

Trick's blood was sweet and thick and life and *Trick*.

His Sweets' scream echoed with his, bouncing off the brick and filling the alley with their need, their joy as Trick shook in his arms.

He lost himself in the flavor of his lover, fierce pulls gentling into sweet sucking as his hunger eased, not taking too much, but keeping the pleasure constant between them.

Finally he closed the wound, lapping at Trick's skin, moaning softly.

Trick's hands gentled and began to stroke through his hair. His words were soft, breathless. "Oh, baby-boy. Bast. Love... oh, I needed that. Need you so much."

"Trick." He closed his eyes, lips trailing up to nibble along the strong jaw, Trick's flavor singing through him. "Just didn't want to hurt you, Sweets. Wanted to let you get strong again... oh, fuck, nothing tastes as good as you. Nothing feels like you."

"We'll figure something out, okay? Just not that. I don't want to have to go through that again."

"Okay. Yes. Kiss me." He lifted his head, stretching for Trick's lips, high from the rush of life filling him, making him tremble with energy.

"Not gonna make you ask twice." Trick mumbled the words and then his mouth closed over Bast's, soft and wet and hot.

Bast groaned, pushing up against Trick, hips beginning to rock, a new hunger making itself known.

Trick broke the kiss, separating their lips long enough to mutter "take me home" before closing their mouths together again.

Bast lost himself in the kiss, heat building within him. The sounds of laughter and high heels on concrete brought him back and he took a step away from his lover. He held his hand out and grinned. "Let's go home. I want to feel your skin, taste you, love you, not dry-hump against the wall."

Trick laughed. "One of us isn't dry, baby-boy."

Bast chuckled. "Well, then, Sweets, come home and I'll lick you dry."

Trick's grin was relaxed and easy and Bast had missed it. "Best offer I've had in weeks."

Trick brought Bast's hand up to his mouth and kissed his knuckles.

"Home, Trick. Come home and we'll curl in the bed and make love until morning." Bast cupped Trick's jaw, caressing. "Now, before I get hungry again."

Trick's eyes flared at the mention of feeding again, and he started back toward the street, pulling Bast along with him.

Bast hurried after, laughter and happiness filling him. "So much for self-control being the answer to all questions."

"Self-control is overrated," growled Trick. "I don't want to hear about you and self-control ever again. It was killing me, not being able to feed you."

"You think I like those horrible, dead, cold plastic bags, lover?" Bast shook his head. "I need you, Trick. Need to feel you on my tongue. I... I found myself, half-asleep and dreaming, ready to feed, mouth on your fucking sweet skin..."

Trick's hand tightened on his, nails digging into his skin, and their pace sped, Trick almost running and pulling him along. "Baby-boy, if you don't stop with the seduction talk, I will stop and let you take me right here and now -- on the hood of that God-awful teal Geo."

"Fuck, no! It would clash with my hair!" Bast grinned and began to run.

Chapter Thirteen

He bounced out of the theatre, newly fuchsia hair flying in the stiff wind, trench coat flapping and snapping in the way that only really new vinyl could accomplish. His head was swimming, filled with music and colors and glitter.

Absinthe and corsets and lovely boys and tragedy and utter fucking bliss -- Bast was totally enrapt. The stars were bright and twinkling, or maybe he was just seeing the lights of the theatre -- after a few hits of whisky, it was hard to tell. He waited impatiently for Trick and Rose and Bael to hit the exit door.

If they hurried, they could get tickets for the late-late show and see it *again*.

The three of them were deep in conversation as they came out the door, Rose speaking animatedly and Trick shaking his head.

"What the fuck is romantic about death?"

"It's the tragedy, man. It's the level of connection..." Rose was about to head off on one of her famous lectures on the quality of pain in art, Bast could see it in her eyes. He opened his mouth to interrupt when Bael spoke up, drawling lazily.

"Shit, baby. You just like the way that boy cries. Don't make it more than it is."

Trick laughed and bumped his hip against Bast's. "Hey, now there's something to get your panties damp for -- he is one hot babe. I wouldn't say not to seeing those lips wrapped around my--"

"Oh, now there's a porn video I could get into. Will you need extras?" Bast grinned over at his lover, winking outrageously. "I bet we can get Rose to play. Hell, I bet Bear would do your stand-in work."

He ducked under Trick's arm and hid behind Bael, just avoiding the slap aimed at his ass.

"Come on, lets get out of here before any of our assets freeze off." Trick shoved his hands in his jeans pockets. "And no -- I don't want to see it again -- you go back in that theatre, baby-boy, and you go alone."

"But..." Bast gave Trick his second-best pout, peering over Bael's shoulder, ignoring his friend's chuckles. "They *sing*, Trick."

"Yes, and they sang the first time we saw it. And the second. And the third. I'm not saying it's a shitty movie, Bast -- but I don't want to see it again, not tonight. Wouldn't you rather go dancing or out for some coffee or home to fuck?"

"Oooh! Trick! You said Bast's favorite word!" Rose's eyes were twinkling.

"Yeah. 'Coffee.'" Bael inserted, right on cue.

"I'm so abused!" Bast laughed and headed back towards Trick, sliding in between his lover and Rose easily, enjoying their warmth. "I'm easy, Sweets. The night is young and I've got nothing planned. I'm all yours."

"Now you've said my favorite words." Trick smiled down at him, warmth in his eyes. "How about some dancing? Like a warm up to the fucking."

Bast grinned back, nodding happily. "Yeah, Sweets. Sounds like a blast. Where to? The Zodiac? The Pit? Haven?"

"Depends." Trick's arm slid around his shoulder and his voice dropped, low and intimate. "You need a snack, baby-boy?"

"Sweets..." As always, those words sent a thrill through him, stripping him down from bright-eyed nightchild to sheer, hard-hot hunger. He was addicted -- just as hooked as the too-thin, hollow-eyed kids shooting up in the alleyways.

His eyes roamed over Trick's lean body, nostrils flaring as he breathed in Trick's scent. Of course, what he was hooked on was much more dangerous than smack.

"Let's head to Haven." Trick said aloud before whispering in his ear. "We'll go hide in their back room and let you feed and then go out and dance."

Bast nodded, shivering slightly. Movie, music, friends, the stars -- they all fled his mind in the wake of his hunger.

"You sure know how to capture our Bast's attention, Trick. Hell, you can even make him almost quiet." Rose teased gently, sliding her arm around Bast's waist and squeezing as they headed down the street to the club. "What's your secret?"

"Sex."

Rose cackled. "Oh, fuck, Trick if you're good enough in the sack to keep Bast starry-eyed and quiet, come home with me for a few days? Bear's been on the road touring for weeks."

"But then you'd be spoiled for it and when he got home you'd be disappointed."

Bast grinned, winking over at Rose. "Guess you'll just have to wait for the big guy, mijita. Unless you can tempt our pretty Bael into your lair, of course."

The bouncer at the door smiled at them, friendly and pleasant. "Now here's a troupe I haven't seen in ages! Hey Bast, Bael, Trick. Rose! When are you going to play a gig here? Mike's been asking after you."

Money changed hands and they entered the dark, cavernous club, Bael and Rose heading off to talk to the owner. The music was almost a living thing here, prowling around them like a wild predator.

He turned to Trick, body already taken by the music, hips pressing close. "Hey, Sweets."

"Mm, baby-boy." Trick's hips fit against his, mouth coming down to plunder his. "Back room, Bast. Need your bite."

Bast shuddered, almost coming in his pants right there on the dance floor. He nodded, knowing Trick would see his need, see his hunger and feed on it. They moved together around the dance floor, moving to the door along the back wall, painted to blend in seamlessly.

As soon as they were through it, Trick had him pressed up against the wall, mouth ravaging his, body tight and hot and hard against him.

He could feel Trick's hands, shaking, as his Sweets worked at getting his jeans undone.

Bast was panting, mouth watering as he slid his hands beneath Trick's t-shirt, tracing the quivering muscles, the hard points of nipples, the indentation of navel. His voice left him in a low growl, pleading and needy and feral. "Mm... hungry, Sweets. Hungry for you."

"I know, baby-boy, I know. Suck me -- bite my cock, Bast, make me come." Trick's voice was hoarse, his hands pushing at Bast's shoulders.

"Yes." He slid down the wall, lips covering the tip of Trick's cock. Sucking strongly, he relaxed his throat, taking his lover into him in one smooth motion.

The music pounded around them, throbbing inside his head. He moved with the rhythm, sucking determinedly, purposely keeping his teeth from the hot flesh, purposely making them both wait for what they needed.

"Shit." Trick's hands slid into his hair, pulling, hips moving to fuck his mouth. "Bast..."

Bast hummed, hands cupping Trick's ass. He pulled Trick deep into his throat. He swallowed, biting down at the base, blood splashing over his tongue. Trick's scream ran counter to the driving beat of the music, his come spilling down Bast's throat, mingling with the blood.

He sucked, feeding himself on his lover, filling his need and sating his hunger.

Trick's hands were tight in his hair, his Sweets leaning on him, making, soft, happy noises.

Long after Trick was clean, wound healed beneath his tongue, Bast sucked and licked and laved, enjoying the feel and flavor of his lover in his mouth.

Finally he leaned back, letting the warm, sweet flesh slide free, kissing the tip gently before standing.

Trick's mouth found his immediately, hands sliding to cup his cheeks. His Sweets' body was heavy and limp against him.

"Love you, Bast."

"Mm... I love you, Sweets." Bast purred happily, his cheek stroking against Trick's. Every time they said it, it felt easier, more and more right. He pressed closer, the beat of the music reasserting itself in his head. "Wanna dance?"

"You mean make love standing and in public. Oh yeah, baby-boy, I do." Trick's hips moved slowly against his, the sound of jeans against vinyl just barely audible beneath the pounding beat.

Bast's arms twined around his neck, moving against Trick's instinctively. Body loose and fluid, he undulated, eyes closed as he focused only on the beat and the feel of his lover's heat.

They danced through two songs before Trick nuzzled at his neck. "We'd better head back out to the dance floor before Rose and Bael send a search party."

"Oh, yeah." Bast moaned softly, head falling back at Trick's touch. "Dancing with you makes me forget, Sweets."

Trick nibbled at his neck, shoving him hard against the wall. "Fuck, Bast, I want you again."

"So soon?" Bast arched, rubbing himself against Trick's thigh in time to the music, balls tight and aching. The lips against his throat were driving him mad, making him whimper. "You want me here, Sweets? I'm yours."

In answer, Trick's hands slid beneath his coat, sliding it over his shoulders. Bast shrugged it off, leaving him writhing before Trick in low-slung leather pants and a sheer white shirt, unbuttoned to his waist. Trick's hands slid over his shoulders, hot enough to brand, almost as hot as Trick's lips.

His Sweets' thumbs scrapped across his nipples as Trick's knee pushed between his thighs, spreading his legs. He opened for Trick willingly, eagerly, a low wail leaving him as electricity shot from his nipples to his cock, leaving a steady, persistent throbbing behind.

His own hands slid over Trick's cheeks, jaw, the long line of throat. He pressed against the thick vein that pulsed there, just enough that he could feel Trick's heartbeat, enough for Trick to remember the sweet pleasure Bast gave him.

Moaning, Trick turned his head, nipping at Bast's wrist and then licking his skin. Trick's hands slid down, pushing into his pants.

"Oh, fuck, Sweets. You make me ache." He turned Trick's face, licking at the sweet, full open lips. "Taste so good, love, so fucking good."

Trick's tongue slid out to move against his, hot and wet and eager. Their bodies were moving to the music, Trick's hips pushing him back against the wall with the beat.

His lips captured Trick's tongue, pulling, sucking in tandem with the roll of their hips. Bast hooked his knee around Trick's hip, using the leverage to get more friction, more sensation.

The world was shrinking, dissolving into heavy bass and hard cocks and sweet tongues and the overwhelming beat of Trick's pulse.

Trick's hands slid between their bodies, buttons popping and zippers sliding down, their cocks pressing hard and slick against each other, making everything suddenly more. Hands found his shoulders again, holding him tight against the wall, fingers biting into his skin.

Bast cried out, eyes open and wide, staring into his lover. He couldn't get enough, couldn't stop this hunger -- not just for blood. He wanted Trick's cock, Trick's lips, Trick's heart and soul and future and... "Oh, shit, Sweets. Need you."

"Got me, Bast. Anything you want."

He lifted his head for another kiss, unable to find words -- not even "please." His hips were grinding, so close to coming that his body was already convulsing with the bright shocks of pleasure.

Trick's mouth covered his, a sob throbbing between their lips, tongues sharing the vibrations.

He came at the first touch of Trick's tongue to his, his entire body given up in the pursuit of satisfaction. The music's bright notes shattered behind his eyes, golds and blues that looked like Trick, looked like fucking and pleasure and love.

Heat splashed between them, the smell strong and pure.

Another series of bone-deep shudders rocked him, Bast holding onto Trick as his body tried to decide whether to dissolve or shake apart. Trick held him tight against the wall, hands still hard on his shoulders, like an anchor. His Sweets' forehead rested against his own, sharp gasps filling his mouth with his lover's breath.

"Wow." He looked up into dazed eyes, almost black in the darkness.

"Fuck, yeah." Trick shuddered against him, body shivering.

They rested together, blanketed by music and the warmth of their bodies. Finally Bast gathered himself long enough to grin. "I think that counted as three, Sweets. At least."

Trick chuckled and gave him a soft, tender kiss that made them both shiver again. "Come on, baby-boy, let's slip out the back -- I'm taking you home."

"Mm... sounds perfect." He leaned forward, nuzzling Trick's neck gently as he reached down to fasten his pants. "Take me home, Sweets."

Trick's hands were already there, tenderly tucking him back in and zipping him up before taking care of his own. Trick bent, picking up his coat and helping him back into it, closing it across his wet belly and then taking his hand. "Ready, baby-boy?"

"For you? Always, Trick. Always."

His mouth was taken in a quick, searing kiss, and then Trick was pulling him across the room. The fire alarm sounded as Trick pushed open the emergency door and they ran, laughing into the night as they left the club behind them.

End.

Printed in the United States
105728LV00004B/256/A